"Last scoop of ice cream," Daisy said. "You want it?"

"Wouldn't touch it," Steve said. "You eat the last scoop of ice cream, and you're destined to be an old maid. My aunt Zena says so."

Daisy ate the last scoop and set the carton aside. "I don't have an aunt Zena, so it doesn't count for me."

"It counts for everyone. You're in big trouble."

She smiled. "I like to live dangerously. I take my chances."

His eyes shifted to her mouth, and she could feel desire growing between them. It felt like a thunderstorm growing on the horizon. He was going to kiss her, and this time there'd be nothing to stop it from turning into something serious.

"I should go home, do some studying," she said.

"What about living dangerously?" he asked, tugging on a curl. "What about taking chances?"

"I think I've tested the Fates enough for one night," she said softly.

"Let me tell you what Aunt Zena says about missed opportunities," he whispered into her hair. Then she felt him kiss her just below her ear, felt his lips working their way around to her mouth, felt his hand slide under her skimpy T-shirt. She knew she could stop him . . . and she knew she wouldn't. Daisy wanted to be loved. She was hungry for it. More than hungry—she was starved. . . .

WHAT ARE *LOVESWEPT* ROMANCES?

They are stories of true romance and touching emotion. We believe those two very important ingredients are constants in our highly sensual and very believable stories in the *LOVESWEPT* line. Our goal is to give you, the reader, stories of consistently high quality that may sometimes make you laugh, sometimes make you cry, but are always fresh and creative and contain many delightful surprises within their pages.

Most romance fans read an enormous number of books. Those they truly love, they keep. Others may be traded with friends and soon forgotten. We hope that each *LOVESWEPT* romance will be a treasure—a "keeper." We will always try to publish

LOVE STORIES YOU'LL NEVER FORGET
BY AUTHORS YOU'LL ALWAYS REMEMBER

The Editors

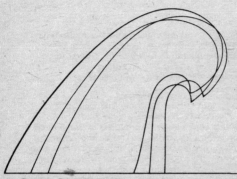

LOVESWEPT® · 460

Janet Evanovich
The Rocky Road to Romance

BANTAM BOOKS

NEW YORK · TORONTO · LONDON · SYDNEY · AUCKLAND

THE ROCKY ROAD TO ROMANCE
A Bantam Book / March 1991

Published simultaneously in the United States and Canada

PRINTED IN THE UNITED STATES OF AMERICA

OPM   0 9 8 7 6 5 4 3 2 1

Prologue

At six-thirty A.M., when Washington, D.C., was waking to another sweltering summer day, a Ledbetter Oil Company tank truck rolled off a ramp of the capital beltway, spilling five hundred gallons of highly flammable black gunk across four lanes of traffic. No one was injured, but the rush-hour commuters traveling the outer loop found themselves in hopeless gridlock surpassing even the normal snarl of morning traffic.

As operations manager of WZZZ, AM radio, Steve Crow didn't wish bad luck on anyone, but in his eyes, thanks to Ledbetter Oil Company this had all the makings of a superior Monday. It was now nine-thirty in the morning, and Ledbetter's gunk was still being sanded, shoveled, and scrubbed off the beltway, trapping half of Northern Virginia in transit. The nation's movers and shakers were sweating and swearing in their cars, and each and every one of them was tuned to WZZZ. WZZZ told the news, all the news, and nothing but the news—twenty-four hours a day. And while some detractors of AM radio felt the call letters prophetic, no one caught in Washington's daily commuter crunch could deny the pull of WZZZ's traffic report. Sooner or later, if you sat in traffic long enough, you tuned to WZZZ. During rush hours WZZZ kept a helicopter aloft, giving live traffic reports every fifteen minutes. The worse the traffic, the higher WZZZ climbed on the ratings charts—and today's traffic was gloriously terrible.

Steve Crow was celebrating with a jelly doughnut, chewing happily, watching in fatalistic resignation as powdered sugar sifted onto his navy slacks. When a glob of jelly plopped onto his striped power tie, he muttered an expletive and yanked at the knot.

His secretary stopped by his open office door and shook her head when she saw him. "You get jelly doughnut on your tie again? How many does that make this month? Everybody knows you do it on purpose so you don't have to wear a tie, so why don't you just leave it at home?"

"Wouldn't look good. I'm a professional person."

"You're a professional weirdo," his secretary said. "Good thing for you you're so good at what you do."

"Mmmm, and I'm cute too," Steve said.

"Cute? Let me tell you . . . puppies are cute, panties that say Tuesday are cute, and drinks that come with little paper umbrellas are cute. You are *not* cute. You are wickedly handsome."

He grinned and washed the doughnut down with half a cup of coffee. "Give yourself a raise, Charlene. And get me this week's advertising schedule when you get a chance."

"Work, work, work," she said, then turned to march off to the copier. "I thought this was gonna be a glamour job. Get dressed up, meet some celebrities . . ."

Steve slouched in his chair and looked through the large glass window that separated him from his staff. He watched the anchor move through his cue cards, manipulating his tape carts and controls in a glassed-in booth at the far side of the room. The editor and the assistant editor sat at their console outside the broadcast booth. Reporters worked at consoles lined against the inside wall. Everything was cranking along perfectly. Steve smiled in satisfaction, flipping the switch to pipe the broadcast into his office.

Frank Menken, the midday traffic reporter, had just been cued in. From nine to four when the traffic job wasn't usually as critical, Menken took over the traffic car without the aid of a helicopter team. He drove a circular route around the city, relying on three scanners with a hundred bands apiece, a CB, a two-way radio, a car phone, and an AM radio equipped with an earplug. It was a grueling job that required being able to listen, talk, drive, and drink coffee, all at the same time.

"Traffic heavy on the G.W. Parkway due to construction," Menken said, broadcasting as he drove. "We've got a minor delay on the approach to the Whitehurst Freeway. There's been a three-car collision but police are on the scene and no one seems to be hurt. Prince George's County reports . . ."

There was a pause in Menken's rapid-fire recitation, and then Menken suddenly launched into vigorous, unexpected swearing. Steve Crow jumped to his feet; the editor immediately cut Menken off the air, and the newsroom was filled with the crackle of static coming from Menken's two-way radio. Just one word made its way through the static.

"—Garbage!" Menken gasped, and then all was silent.

One

Daisy Adams was an enterprising twenty-six-year-old graduate student. She'd written a cookbook called *Bones for Bowser,* and somehow, through sheer tenacity, she'd managed to turn a gimmick into a five-minute slot on WZZZ every Monday morning. She filled her air time with dog stories and gave detailed directions on how to make homemade dog biscuits, dog soup, and dog stew. She'd become the darling of the morning DJs on the FM stations who made her the brunt of their jokes, referring to her as the "Dog Lady of Snore," hitting on a tender subject for Steve Crow and his unfortunate luck in call letters.

A few wisps of bangs straggled over her forehead, tortoise-shell combs held her blond hair swept back from her temples, and big, loose curls tumbled in a luxuriant mass down the back of her head and neck to an inch below her shoulders. Her eyes were big and blue, her nose small, her mouth wide. She had a gamine quality to her face that was completely misleading because there wasn't an ounce of gamine in her personality. Her ex-boyfriend had compared her to Attila the Hun, but most people thought she was more like an upscale version of the Little Engine That Could.

At ten-fifteen Daisy swung into the newsroom. She waved hello to the anchor in the glass booth and gave the Capitol Hill correspondent a bag of experimental snacks for his beagle. She adjusted the strap on her oversized shoulder bag and dropped into a seat beside the editor. "What happened to Frank? I heard him giving the traffic report while I was driving in. He said a rude word and that was the last of him."

"Rear-ended a garbage truck and got buried under half a ton of dumpster droppings. He's okay except for a broken leg."

Daisy pulled a five-by-seven card from her pocketbook and glanced over a recipe for dog granola. "That's too bad. Who's doing traffic?"

"Nobody's doing traffic. Steve's offered double Frank's salary plus a year's supply of Girl Scout cookies, but nobody'll take it."

Daisy felt her heart jump. *Double Frank's salary!* "I could do it," she said. "I need the money."

"You need money that bad?"

She bit her lower lip to keep herself under control. This was the chance of a lifetime. She had enormous school expenses, a big rent payment due, a live-in little brother who was eating her out of house and home, and a car that drank a quart of motor oil a week. She was determined to make it on her own. Besides her dog lady job, she worked as a school crossing guard, a waitress on the eleven-to-two lunch shift at Roger's Steak House, and delivered newspapers. She'd written *Bones for Bowser* to give herself additional income, but she wasn't due a royalty check for three more months. If she took the traffic job, she could drop waitressing. Maybe she could even give up the newspaper route. She was doing the dissertation for her doctorate and she could work on it at night.

She swiveled in her seat and looked across the room at Steve Crow. She'd always been a little frightened of him. With his jet-black hair, dark piercing eyes, slightly aquiline nose, he was an intimidating figure. His complexion was dark, his shoulders broad, his hips narrow. The scuttlebut at the station said his father was pure-blood American Indian; his mother was Hispanic.

Nervously, Daisy waved at him with just the tips of her fingers. He scowled back and immediately averted his eyes to some pressing piece of business on his desk. She sighed. Stubborn, she thought. She'd nagged him for a month before he gave her the five-minute Bowser spot. She wondered what she'd have to do to get the traffic job.

Nothing ventured nothing gained, she told

herself, pushing the hair out of her eyes. She might as well give it a try. "Excuse me," she said, knocking on Crow's open door. "I'd like to talk to you about the job of traffic reporter. I'd like to apply for it . . . just until Frank's leg is better. I wouldn't want to steal his job. Even if I was wonderful, which I'm sure I'll be, I still wouldn't expect you to keep me on. Actually, the timing is perfect because I'll get a royalty check in three months and then hopefully I won't need so many jobs."

Steve looked beyond her, to his secretary eavesdropping through the glass window. He watched Charlene mouth the word "perfect" to him, watched her eyes fill with suppressed laughter. He lifted an eyebrow and she scuttled away.

Perfectly awful, he thought. Putting Daisy Adams in the WZZZ traffic car was like committing broadcasting suicide. The woman was cute, but her specialty was baking dog biscuits, for crying out loud. True, she received more fan mail than everyone else combined, but that was one of those freak things. She was entertaining. Kind of earnest and goofy all at the same time. Unfortunately, he had no other option. He'd gone through six traffic reporters in the past year trying to find a backup. At least she wouldn't be doing rush hour, he told himself. How bad could she be?

Without waiting for his reply, Daisy added, "And don't worry about my *Bones for Bowser* spot. I can do it on the road!"

He managed a small smile. "Terrific."

Ten minutes later they were in the Shulster Building parking garage.

"Wow!" Daisy said, looking at the station's auxiliary newscar. "It's got enough antennae to get Mars. This is going to be incredible. I think I'm going to like this." She cracked her knuckles, looked up into Steve Crow's face, and felt a shiver run along her spine. She wasn't a shy sort of person, and she wasn't usually uncomfortable with men. She could tick off on one hand the things that truly made her nervous: the dentist, signing her name to her income tax statement, looking in her rearview mirror and seeing a police cruiser—and Steve Crow. Standing next to Steve Crow was like taking fifteen volts of electricity. He made her feel like her scalp was smoking.

Steve unlocked the car and opened the passenger side door for Daisy. "I don't have any meetings until one o'clock, so I'll ride the loop with you. I'll do the talking and driving for the first hour and then you can take over."

An hour alone in the newscar with Steve Crow? She'd die. Her heart would stop beating. "That's really not necessary. Not at all. I mean, I hate to take you away from whatever it is that you do. Probably you could just give me a few notes and a full tank of gas and send me on my way."

"You look kind of flushed," Steve said. "You sure you feel okay? You aren't sick, are you?"

"It's you. You make me nervous."

"You mean because I'm your boss? Don't

worry about it. Your *Bowser* spot is secure. Those people out there in radio land love you."

"I know."

"You do?"

"I get a lot of fan mail," Daisy said. "And last week I was invited to be on *Good Morning America*."

"So what's the problem?"

"I don't know. Isn't that weird? You're just sort of scary. I think it might be something chemical."

He was standing very close to her. Close enough to see the fine texture of her skin, close enough to see that her hair was silky and thick, close enough to see the pulse beating erratically in her neck . . . close enough to be getting a trifle uncomfortable himself. But unlike Daisy, who seemed to be a little vague about her discomfort, he knew for certain exactly where his originated.

"Maybe we just got off on the wrong foot," he said. "I have to admit, in the beginning I didn't see much value in the station running recipes for dogs." In the beginning he hadn't noticed her big blue eyes—eyes the color of cornflowers. And in the beginning he hadn't felt this compelling urge to kiss her, to slide his hand under her shirt and feel her smooth warm skin against his palm. In the beginning he'd been a sane, rational human being. And what was he now? Now he was a man lusting after a woman who baked dog cookies. He wondered how that could have happened in such a short amount of time. One minute she was a thorn in his side and the next minute she was a lump in his throat and an ache in his groin.

Daisy saw his gaze drop from her eyes to her mouth, and she felt her blood pressure inch up a notch. This was ridiculous, she thought. She'd allowed herself to become positively unglued over Steve Crow's high cheekbones and deep, dark eyes. She needed to put things back into perspective. She didn't even know him! She searched for an appropriate remark. "I'm afraid I might have been pushy about getting airtime."

"You were the most annoying, most persistent person ever to darken my door."

"I was a woman with a cause."

"That'll do it," Steve said. "I hope you don't mind my asking, but I've always wondered if you made these dog recipes yourself. Do you stay up late making dog soup and bacon dog burgers?"

"I never gave a recipe for bacon dog burgers!"

"You know what I mean."

"Some of it's serious. Americans lavish a great deal of time and money and affection on their pets. Sometimes I think it's because of the disappearance of the extended family. We're substituting dogs and cats and hamsters for aunts and uncles and grandparents. And when someone considers a pet as a member of the family, they start to become more concerned with its health and nutrition. I don't think there are many people out there slaving over my recipes for dog granola, but I think some of them pay attention to the advice I give about a balanced canine diet. And I think some of them bake their own dog biscuits once in a while just because it's a fun project for kids. And I think *lots* of people are listening to me because I'm pop entertainment. I've become sort of a fad."

So not only did she smell great, Steve thought, but she was perceptive too. Why hadn't he noticed that sooner? He plunged his hands into his pockets and rocked back on his heels. "What about your motives? Do you have a dog? Do you feed him homemade liver soup?"

Daisy smiled. She was beginning to feel more comfortable around him. "My motives are terrible. I did it for money. I thought the book would be a novelty item and help me get through my last couple years of school."

Her smile just about knocked him over. It was a wide, generous smile that tipped up at the corners of her mouth and warmed his stomach. If his hands hadn't been stuffed into his pockets, he would have traced a fingertip along her lower lip. "What are you studying?"

She leaned against the car. "Psych. My specialty is geriatric psychology."

She had a soft spot in her heart for dogs and old people. Steve thought that was nice. He wondered how she felt about minorities. Probably, she loved minorities. He was a shoo-in, he decided. He'd buy a dog, introduce her to his grandparents, and then show her his bedroom.

"We should get going," she said. "Everyone's probably waiting for a traffic report." She was eager to start her new job, and she was beginning to feel uncomfortable again. She preferred to have Steve Crow's disturbing brown eyes trained on something other than her. She edged her way past him and slunk down into the passenger seat. "What are all these gizmos?" she asked, patting the dashboard.

Steve moved to the driver's side and slid behind the wheel, taking a fast survey of the equipment. "You have three scanners, a two-way radio, car phone . . . " He fiddled with the scanners. "It's been a lot of years since I've done a traffic report."

"I didn't know you were a traffic reporter."

He turned the key in the ignition and backed out of the parking space. "I've done just about everything there is to do in radio. I started as an intern when I was still in high school and over the years I've worked my way around the newsfloor."

"Came up the hard way, huh?"

"Not exactly. My dad owned a radio station."

"Oh."

He paused for a minute on the off ramp while he blinked in the sudden glare of noon-hour sun. "You sound disappointed."

"No. Just surprised. I've never met anyone whose father owned a radio station."

Steve shrugged. "The ancestral land turned out to have lots of oil. Several years ago my dad was told to diversify his holdings and communication was an area that appealed to him."

"Does he own WZZZ?"

"No. He owns a network in the Southwest. When I got out of college I decided I wanted to make my own success, so I stayed on the East Coast." Steve called in to the studio on the two-way radio to let the editor know he was on the road and would be broadcasting. "Every fifteen minutes you get a sixty-second spot," he told Daisy. "You watch the clock on the dash and when you're coming up to newstime you use the headset to listen for your cue from the anchor." He clicked the scanners on and showed her how to use them to get the priority channels. "We'll take Route 66 to the beltway and then head north. We want to avoid the oil spill on the outer loop. You *always* want to avoid traffic." He looked at the clock. It was eight minutes after eleven. He turned the volume down on the scanners and put the earplug in his ear. "This is Steve Crow giving you the WZZZ traffic report," he said into the two-way radio. "Hazmat teams are still on the scene of that oil spill on the Braddock Road off ramp, but traffic is finally moving around it. Keep to the two left lanes—"

Daisy felt a jolt of fear hit her stomach. Steve was doing fifty, weaving in and out of traffic, broadcasting live, talking off the top of his head, cramming as much information as was possible into a sixty-second slot. Daisy stared at him openmouthed, wondering how he'd managed to make a newscast out of the squawking coming off the scanners. And she was wondering how *she* was going to do it. She needed notes to relay a dog-food recipe! And if that wasn't problem enough, she was uncoordinated. She couldn't chew gum and drive at the same time. What was she thinking of? *Money,* she reminded herself—that's what she was thinking of. Pure unbridled greed had led her to the WZZZ traffic car.

Steve gave his name and call letters, removed the earphone, and put the two-way radio back into its cradle. "It's really not so bad," he said. "A good memory helps and you need to be able to talk fairly fast, giving continuous information."

"No problem," Daisy said. "This doesn't look too tough. I can do this." Daisy, Daisy, Daisy, she silently screamed, stick with waitressing! Keep the newspaper route!

For the next hour they drove north on the beltway, passing from Northern Virginia into Maryland, and then south toward the Woodrow Wilson Bridge. Daisy concentrated on the scanners and tried composing traffic reports in her mind. She was used to talking on the radio—at least she had that going for her, she thought. She didn't usually feel stage fright.

At six minutes to twelve Steve handed Daisy an auxiliary earplug and the handset for the two-way. "I'll keep driving. You do the talking this time."

She felt her throat constrict and her eyes glaze over. Her mind went blank. The sound of the anchor cuing in the traffic report came loud and clear through the earplug. The anchor repeated the cue and Steve tapped Daisy on the top of the head with a rolled-up newspaper that had been lying on the front seat.

"This is Daisy Adams," she said. "WZZZ traffic at eleven fifty-five." There was a long pause while she bit her lip. Steve hit her on the head again and she snatched the newspaper from him while she frantically groped for something to say. "Traffic is . . . um, the same as before," she finally said. "If you listened fifteen minutes ago, then you pretty much know what's going on. Stay tuned for an update. We'll let you know if the traffic changes. This is Daisy Adams signing off."

There was a pause about four heartbeats long before the anchor resumed broadcasting. The man's voice sounded strangled, and Steve had a horrifying image of the entire newsroom doubled over with laughter.

"Oh my Lord," Daisy said. "I couldn't think of anything to say!"

Steve noticed his knuckles were white as he gripped the wheel. Relax, he told himself. It's not the end of the world. It's not nuclear war. It's not famine in Ethiopia. It's just a one-minute traffic report. And this was an emergency situation. Besides, she'd probably be fine. She just needed more time. When they were done driving the loop he'd park her somewhere and let her listen to the scanners. The next time she could take notes and read from them when her airtime came up.

Two

At twelve-thirty Steve pulled into the Belle Haven Marina parking lot. He faced the news-car toward the Potomac River, giving Daisy a view of grassy parkland, the river, and the Woodrow Wilson Bridge that joined Virginia and Maryland.

"It isn't necessary for us to do any more driving," he said to Daisy. "We've checked out all the trouble spots. You get good scanner reception here and you're free from interference on the two-way. You have a good view of bridge traffic. It's the perfect place to wait out the afternoon." It was the perfect place to roll around in the grass like cats in heat, he thought. That's how he felt—like a battle-scarred tom that had finally found the love of his life. He wanted to crawl into the backseat and yowl. But he didn't think Daisy was ready for his yowling, and besides, he had meetings all afternoon, so he squashed his animal instincts and used the car phone to call for a cab.

While he waited, he leaned his back against the driver's side door, stretched his long legs as best he could in the compact, and draped an arm over the steering wheel. He didn't want to leave yet. He wanted time to get to know her better. And he wanted to stay and help with the traffic report. It wasn't fair to throw her into this job and abandon her after less than two hours of instruction. "Are you going to be able to handle this?"

Their gazes locked and she knew he needed an honest answer. "I'm not going to give up on it, if that's what you're asking."

"That was part of it."

"And the other part? I suppose that has to do with ability. I'll be able to do a decent traffic report after a few days. Just don't expect me to sound like Menken." Daisy thought the key word there was "decent." She was going to give it her best shot, but she didn't think traffic was ever going to be her forte.

Shaking his head, Steve walked away.

She watched him, then looked at the bridge in the distance. The cars crawling across it seemed like tiny toys. A small boat made its way upriver, a man and a woman sat eating lunch at a nearby picnic table, two cyclists skimmed along the black-topped bike trail in front of the car. The air coming through the open windows was warm, carrying with it the smell of grass baking in the sun.

An hour and a half earlier she'd been afraid to be alone in a car with Steve. Now she was scared to death to have him leave. He still looked very much the predator with his dark, sensual eyes and sleek muscled body, but he'd been a perfect gentleman all morning. He'd been patient and polite and extremely helpful. Just proved how deceiving looks can be, she told herself. Never judge a book by its cover. Steve Crow obviously didn't have a lecherous bone in his body—at least not where she was concerned.

Daisy had her head in the freezer compartment of her refrigerator when her fourteen-year-old brother tapped her on the shoulder.

"There's a lecher at the door," Kevin Adams announced. "He says he's come to see you."

Daisy stopped foraging for supper. She withdrew from the freezer with a bag of french-fried potato balls and a plastic tray of chicken nuggets. "A lecher?"

"You probably think I'm given to exaggeration, but I know a lecher when I see one. And this guy has a big-bucks car. A sexy two-seater foreign job. Long and low and black. Man, would I ever like to have a car like that. I tell you, his car is evil. It could probably get airborne."

Daisy walked into the foyer and found Steve Crow standing on her front porch. He was holding several bags, and he smiled at her through the screen door.

"Decided I needed to tell you some more things about the job," he said. He held the bags up for her inspection. "I know I'm coming unannounced at an awkward time, so I brought supper."

"Supper?" Kevin said to Daisy. "Maybe he's not so bad, after all. Besides, you could probably use a lecher in your life. I know I sure as heck could use some food in mine."

Daisy rolled her eyes. Her little brother drank a gallon of orange juice and a gallon of milk a day. It took him two days to go through a loaf of bread and a jar of peanut butter, fifteen minutes to eat a half-gallon of ice cream, twenty minutes to eat a chicken, and if she bought a pie it was gone before she had a chance to take the rest of the groceries out of the bag. "Don't you ever think about anything except food?"

"Sure. I think about girls. That's why I eat so much—substitute gratification. I have all this nervous energy. Us fourteen-year-olds are just a hotbed of hormonal activity. That's how come I'm so good at recognizing a lecher. I figure if I work hard enough at it, I could grow up to be a lecher someday."

Daisy grimaced at her brother and opened the door to Steve. "This is very nice of you. I was just about to defrost something." She motioned to Kevin. "This is my brother Kevin. He's staying with me while my parents are away. My dad is being transferred to San Antonio and my parents are in Texas house-hunting."

"Boss car," Kevin said.

Steve could see the family resemblance. Same blond hair and blue eyes. Same nose, same wide smile. That was where the similarity stopped. Kevin was all gangly arms and legs and he had feet that looked like they belonged on Bozo the Clown. Fourteen or fifteen, Steve guessed. The hungry age. Steve decided to change his strategy for the evening. He handed Kevin a bag. "You like ribs?"

"We're gonna be friends," Kevin said. "What are your intentions about my sister? Are you going to marry her?"

"Not on an empty stomach," Steve said. "One thing at a time." He gave Kevin the other two bags. "Biscuits and coleslaw and frozen yogurt," he told Kevin. "And they're all yours. I'm going to take your sister on a field trip. We'll eat out." He looked at Daisy. "Is that okay? Did you have plans for this evening?"

"I was going to the library. . . ."

"She always goes to the library," Kevin said. "She's a real brain. She rented this place because it's near a library. Can you believe it?"

"I don't have much time," Daisy said. "I try to be efficient."

Steve took the bags of frozen food from her and stuffed them into the crook of Kevin's arm. "Put these back into the freezer."

"So what kind of field trip is this?" Kevin asked.

"I work at WZZZ. Daisy's taken over the job of traffic reporter, and I wanted to show her how to use the portable equipment."

"Awesome."

"I won't be late," Daisy said to Kevin. "Don't blast the neighbors out of their houses with the stereo. Mrs. Schnable just had a hysterectomy and needs her rest."

She stopped midway to the car and stared. Kevin had been right—it did look a little evil. And it looked very expensive. "Nice car," she said.

Steve nodded. "It's transportation." Did she buy that? It was a toy, and he knew it. He'd bought it on a whim and had regretted it ever since. It attracted weird women. Women left their phone numbers attached to his windshield wipers. Sometimes he found panties draped over his antenna. And one time he'd returned from grocery shopping to find a woman had handcuffed herself to his grille. His next car was going to be a Jeep, he'd decided. Women probably didn't handcuff themselves to Jeeps.

They got in the car and drove to a Mexican restaurant close to Daisy's subdivision. Steve took a small leather rucksack from the backseat and carried it inside with him. When they were seated in a booth and had given their order, he said, "I forgot to tell you about the portable scanner this afternoon." He took it from the rucksack and handed it to her. "If you have to leave the newscar for *any* reason, you should carry this with you. It's very similar to the scanners mounted on your dash. Just pull the antenna up and you're all set to go."

Daisy noticed there was something else in the leather bag. She slid her hand in and withdrew a small tape recorder. "What's this for?"

"It's nothing. You don't have to worry about that."

"It must be here for a reason . . ."

Steve mentally cussed himself out. In his haste to see Daisy he'd forgotten to remove the recorder. In some ways WZZZ was the last bastion of old-fashioned reporting. Most of the programming was done live, and because they had a newscar circling the city they were often first on the scene of a fast-breaking story. Menken could reach the site of a plane crash or a Metro accident quickly, use the recorder for an on-scene interview, and broadcast the recorded interview from his car. But Menken was a seasoned reporter, as was the rush-hour team. Daisy Adams was not.

He searched for another purpose for the recorder. "You could use it to prerecord your one-minute slot, but I don't think that will be necessary. Your reports later today sounded fine." Actually, they were terrible, but he wasn't completely stupid. He didn't destroy a fledgling reporter's confidence with harsh criticism, and he didn't insult a woman with cornflower eyes.

Daisy felt like giving a sigh of relief. She'd been afraid he'd taken her to dinner to fire her! And here he was telling her she was fine. She could hardly believe it. "Was I really fine? I was scared to death."

"It was actually unique. It was the first time we've ever had a traffic reporter sign off the air with a recipe for meat loaf."

"I thought people might be getting bored listening to the same old traffic stuff. And it was so depressing. There were accidents and jam-ups everywhere."

He took a few deep breaths and told himself to remain calm. She obviously didn't understand the concept of continuous traffic reporting. It was a natural mistake. He'd have to discuss it with her—sometime when there weren't more pressing subjects of conversation. Sometime when he'd already learned about her favorite color and what kind of music she liked and whether she slept in the nude.

"To tell you the truth, the recipe came from my *Bones for Bowser* cookbook," Daisy said. "Last week my brother accidentally ate some meat loaf I'd made for my neighbor's dog, and he really liked it, so I figured it would be all right to pass along the recipe as people food. Ordinarily I don't have time for cooking, but I cook and dog-test all my Bowser recipes."

The waitress brought a soda for Daisy and a beer for Steve. It was the second time she'd made reference to her lack of time, Steve thought, sipping his beer. He hoped it wasn't a boyfriend that was keeping her so busy. That would complicate his plans. "I suppose graduate school is pretty demanding," he said. "Doesn't leave much time for cooking

and socializing?" He congratulated himself on
being so slick.

"I think I must not be very good at managing my time. I never seem to have enough of
it."

"Maybe I can help. I'm good at time management. You can tell me what you do every day,
and I'll tell you what you're doing wrong."

"I don't know—"

"For instance, what time do you get up in
the morning?"

"I get up at five."

Steve took that under consideration. The
last time he saw five o'clock was four years ago
when there was a fire in the basement of his
apartment building. "Why do you get up so
early?"

"I deliver papers. It takes me two hours to go
through my route. It's a terrific job for people
still in school because you get it over with first
thing in the morning."

"Uh-huh."

"Then after the papers are delivered I go
home and change into my crossing-guard
uniform—"

"Steve blinked. "You're a crossing guard
too?"

"Only in the morning. Last year a little girl
was hurt in my neighborhood because they
didn't have enough crossing guards to cover
all the busy intersections."

"So you volunteered," Steve said.

"It's really fun. The kids are great. During
the regular school year I work at the high

school and then at eight o'clock I go over to Elm and Center Street to cross the grade school kids. Summer school is only in session at the high school right now so I'm done at eight o'clock."

"Gee, what do you do with all that spare time?"

"I used to jog for an hour and then get to work on school stuff, but now that I'm the traffic reporter I'll have to leave for the station at somewhere around eight-fifteen to eight-thirty." She held her hand up. "I know what you're thinking. You're thinking that the traffic job will be too much for me to handle with all my other commitments, but you're wrong. You see, it actually will make things much easier for me. I used to wait tables during lunch and moonlight as a cab driver. I think I can give up those jobs now."

"Cab driver?"

"Actually, I'm terrible. I get lost all the time. Traffic reporting is a snap compared to cab driving."

He narrowed his eyes. "You have any other jobs?"

"No. Well, yes, if you count the internship?"

"What internship?"

"It's part of my doctorate program. I do some recreational counseling at a nursing home."

"You don't have a boyfriend, do you?"

It had been more statement than question, and it took her by surprise. "No. How'd you know that?"

"Lucky guess."

Her eyes widened when the waitress brought what looked like a taco mountain and plunked it down in front of her. "So what do you think?" she asked. "What am I doing wrong?"

"You're overcommitted."

She scooped up a glob of refried beans and taco sauce with a piece of tostado shell. "I've been thinking of giving up the paper route."

Good choice, he thought. The paper route would put a major crimp in his style. It would greatly restrict the early-morning activities he had planned for Daisy. "Definitely. The paper route should go."

They ate in silence for a while until a woman came over to the table and stared at Daisy. "Excuse me, but are you Daisy Adams, author of *Bones for Bowser*? I recognize you from your author photo."

"Yup. That's me," Daisy said with a smile.

"I wouldn't miss your show for anything!" the woman said. "I made your chicken-guts recipe for my dog Sparky and he just loved it. Do you suppose I could have your autograph?"

"Of course. And I'm glad Sparky liked the recipe." Daisy scrawled her name on the woman's napkin.

The waitress sidled up beside the woman. "I couldn't help overhearing. Are you really Daisy Adams? Did you do the traffic report today?"

Daisy nodded her head. "I'm filling in for Frank Menken."

"Well, let me tell you, you were wonderful," the waitress said. "It was the first time I could make anything out of that traffic report. I never knew what that Menken fella was saying. Everything was always so fast and technical. Now when you told us there was an accident by the gas station with the green and yellow trim and the tubs of red geraniums by the gas pumps I knew exactly where you meant."

Steve remembered the broadcast too. That was when he'd sent his secretary out to buy more aspirin.

The waitress patted Daisy's hand. "The dessert's on me, honey. You just have whatever you want."

"Vanilla ice cream," Daisy said. "I need something cool after this taco extravaganza."

The waitress hurried back with a twelve-scoop bowl of vanilla ice cream smothered in strawberries and whipped cream. "We don't often have celebrities here," she said. "This is a real pleasure."

Twenty minutes later the ice cream had been greatly reduced, and what was left was almost completely melted. Steve and Daisy listlessly stared at the carnage.

"I can't eat any more," Daisy said. "I'm getting sick."

Steve let one more spoonful slide down his throat. He had mixed feelings about Daisy's celebrity status. As a businessman he knew he should be loving it. As a newsman he felt a little offended. And as her future lover, he didn't like it at all. He was surprised at that last revelation. He'd never felt possessive about a woman before. It was a lot easier being a modern man when you weren't in lust, he concluded.

He paid the bill and escorted Daisy from the restaurant. When they reached the car there were three pieces of paper attached to his windshield wipers. "Junk mail," he said, removing the notes and instantly crumpling them.

"Don't you want to see what they say?"

"They're phone numbers of women I don't know. It's the car. Women feel compelled to leave their phone number on it."

"How odd."

"Yeah. Sometimes it gets even odder."

The ride home was quiet, giving Daisy time to think about the notes impaled on Steve's windshield wipers. It wasn't the car that drew women, she thought. It was Steve. Most likely those women had seen him park or perhaps drive down the street. Not only was he drop-dead handsome, but he radiated sexual attraction. It was almost impossible to sit across from him and keep her mind on things like ice cream and radio broadcasts. Watching him eat had been torture. Every move he made seemed laced with sensuality. Fire always seemed to smolder behind his dark eyes, and Daisy imagined it was the sort of fire that could sweep across a woman's body and leave her gasping. Part of her was drawn to that fire. Another part of her, the sensible Daisy, said "No way." She was a quiet overachiever who was going to spend the rest of her life counseling senior citizens. Steve Crow would find her boring beyond belief. And she was sure she'd find him overwhelming. Steve Crow belonged with a hot-pink, hot-pants type of woman. Daisy ran more to well-washed denim. Besides that, he was her boss.

It was dark when Steve parked in front of Daisy's town house. The subdivision wasn't exactly run-down, but it wasn't spiffy either, he decided. The homes were small, mostly brick and he guessed about twenty years old. It was a modest neighborhood with small front yards overrun with azaleas and impatiens. Maple trees shaded slightly neglected lawns. Roots snaked beneath sidewalks, causing them to shift and crack. It would be a childless neighborhood, Steve thought, inhabited by singles, newlyweds, and seniors. Families required more space, more yard. Families lived in the nearby subdivisions of colonial houses that had spread like a heat rash through Northern Virginia.

He'd spent the ride home preparing a speech. "Daisy," he'd say, "I have a confession to make. I just used the portable scanner as an excuse to see you. I know this is a little sudden, but the truth is I'm painfully attracted to you, and I need to know, if I try to kiss you, will you consider it job harassment?" It wasn't as if she were a permanent, full-time employee, he reasoned. Her job in the traffic car was temporary. And her dog food slot fell into the free-lance category. He wondered if it would help his cause if he asked her to marry him. Probably, but it might be too soon. He'd give her a few more days on that one. No sense pushing things.

Suddenly the front door to Daisy's house crashed open and Kevin came flying out, followed by a big black dog. Kevin spotted the car, ran up to it, wrenched the door open and jumped in, pushing Daisy over the gearshift, squashing her against Steve Crow. Kevin slammed the door just in time to shut out the dog. The animal snuffled at them through the window and licked the glass.

"Hi," Kevin said. "Have a nice dinner?"

Steve put a protective arm around Daisy, drawing her even closer. "Very nice. How were the ribs?"

"Oh man, the ribs were great."

Daisy felt a thrill race all the way to her toes. Her skin felt scalded where it pressed against Steve Crow. Her stomach tumbled. Her breasts felt swollen and wanting. Her mind went blank. *Daisy*, she silently shouted, *get a grip!* This wasn't sexual groping. This was an innocent scrunching together.

"So what's with the dog?" Steve asked Kevin. "He a friend of yours?"

Kevin's eyes bulged. "I opened the back door to take out the garbage and he lunged at me!"

"It's only Fang," Daisy said. "He belongs to Emily Atkinson two doors down. I don't have a dog so I use him to test my new recipes. Sometimes when he's hungry he finds ingenious ways of getting into my backyard—like digging under the privacy fence."

"I'm telling you, that dog's a killer!" Kevin said.

Daisy leaned forward a little and looked at Fang. "He's just a puppy. He hasn't learned manners yet. He starts obedience school next week."

Kevin wasn't convinced. "I don't like the way he's looking at me."

"You're going to have to get used to him," Daisy said. "He's the only dog in the whole subdivision. I promised my publisher a sequel to *Bones for Bowser* and Fang is my guinea pig."

Steve leaned forward, pretending to look at Fang, but actually finding an excuse not to lose body contact with Daisy. She felt good tucked back against his chest—too good to let go. He looked at Fang and had a stroke of genius. He rested his cheek against Daisy's blond curls and lied to her. "You could use *my* dog."

His voice was low and raspy, whispering through the loose tendrils that had escaped the comb and curled around her ear, and it took her a moment to realize he hadn't said something seductive. She turned to face him and was intrigued by the amused curve to his lips—as if he'd done something very clever and was enormously pleased with himself.

"I didn't know you had a dog," she said.

"Yup. I've got one."

"What's his name?"

Steve stared at her for a full minute. "Bob."

Fang circled the car, snuffled into the window one last time, and left. Everyone watched while he scratched at his door to be let in. Emily Atkinson opened her door and shook her finger at her dog. A moment later, she dragged him in by his collar.

"Bob would be a *real* challenge," Steve said. "He's very finicky."

"What kind of dog is he?" Daisy wanted to know.

"Big. He's a big dog so he has to eat lots of good food. But he's gentle. You'd like him. I could bring him over tomorrow after work."

Daisy really didn't have time. On the other hand, a finicky dog would make a much better guinea pig than Fang-who-ate-everything. And she would like to see more of Steve Crow. She might even be able to find a way to plaster herself against his incredible body for a few minutes. Not that she wanted anything to come of it, but another innocent scrunching wouldn't be too terrible. "Okay," she said, "I have a recipe for stir fry I could try out on him."

"You make the dog food, and I'll bring the people food," Steve said.

"All right!" Kevin gave Steve a high five and got out of the car. "See you around."

"See you around."

By the time Daisy slid over the gearshift Steve was waiting to help her out of the car.

"It's nice of you to offer," she said, "but it

isn't necessary for you to bring dinner tomorrow."

"It's the least I can do. After all, you're going to be slaving away over a great meal for old Fred."

"I thought his name was Bob."

"Yeah. That's what I meant. Bob."

He was a little forgetful. She thought that was endearing. "Well, good night."

"Good night."

Neither of them moved.

A small voice in Steve's head whispered, "Hell, go for it!"

"One more thing," he said to Daisy, taking her by the shoulders. He pulled her forward into the circle of his arms and kissed her. It wasn't a getting-to-know-you kiss. It wasn't at all polite. It was pure passion, deep and hard, right from the beginning. He felt her respond, felt the tip of her tongue against his, and he crushed her closer, leaving no doubt about his future intentions.

When he finally released her and stepped back she noticed his satisfied smile was back in place. "Good night," he said pleasantly. Then he turned on his heel and left.

Daisy touched her lips to see if they'd been singed. "G'night."

Three

Daisy pulled into the Belle Haven Marina parking lot, parked the newscar facing the river, and blew out a long sigh of relief. She'd managed to drive the entire loop without having an accident. She'd even given traffic reports.

Now she slouched against the door, angled her legs across the floor, and closed her eyes, trying to remember the last time she'd been this tense. This morning, on the way to work, she decided. She'd been tense when her car had stalled at the fast-food drive-through and fifteen angry motorists, hungry for their morning coffee and muffins, had piled up behind her. She should have had breakfast at home, but Kevin had eaten all twelve of the pancakes she'd prepared. She made a mental note to stop at the store on the way home from work. She'd also been tense at two in the morning when she woke up in a cold sweat thinking about another evening with Steve Crow, realizing he was coming to visit, and remembering the house was a wreck. The shower-stall door needed the grunge scrubbed away and the living room rug was due for a vacuuming. There were cobwebs on the dining room chandelier, fingerprints on the kitchen cabinets, and if he looked in her oven she'd die. So she'd gotten up and cleaned her bathroom, dusted the chandelier, scoured the cabinets, and said the hell with the oven. As far as she was concerned any man who looked in a woman's oven wasn't worth snake spit anyway.

Exhausted, she dozed off with her forehead resting on the wheel. She'd only slept for a few minutes when she woke with a start. The car phone was ringing.

"Good morning," Steve said. "Just calling to see if everything is okay."

"Yup. Everything is fine." Not counting the heart arrhythmia she got when she thought about the way he'd kissed her.

"I also wanted to make sure our dinner date was still on for tonight."

"Of course," Daisy said. "I'm looking forward to meeting Bob."

"Uh, right. If you run into any problems on the job, be sure to call me."

"Thanks, but things are nice and quiet."

She gave her last report at three fifty-five while she was en route to the radio station. As she was heading north on the George Washington Parkway back to the station, a D.C. police call for backup came over a scanner. The officer was shouting into his two-way, giving his location. Gunfire rattled in the background. It sounded as if there was a firefight going on in the southwest section of the city in an area well-known for drugs and violence. There was a request for an ambulance. One of the officers on the scene had been shot. More gunfire.

It seemed to Daisy that this was the sort of news a radio station should know about, so she called WZZZ's editor and told him about the incident, concluding, "I can hear the gunshots coming over the scanner."

"Where are you?"

"Coming up to the Eighteenth Street bridge."

"Take the bridge, babe. Go for it."

"Go for it? What do you mean 'go for it'?" Daisy asked.

"Go mobile. That's what you've got the tape recorder for. You've got the tape recorder, haven't you?"

"You mean you want *me* to go to report on this? Don't you want to send someone else? Someone with more experience?"

"Hell, no. It'd take too long for anyone else to get there."

Daisy looked overhead, saw the bridge directions flash by, and followed them. "Watch out, Lois Lane," she said. "Here comes Daisy Adams!"

Fifteen minutes later she was driving down

a strange street lined with litter and boarded-up buildings. The scanner was still tuned to D.C. police. The confrontation had quieted down. Swat teams were at the site and had a lone gunman pinned down in a row house. The gunman held a little girl hostage. It was a standoff.

A large TV news truck blocked off part of the road, and Daisy felt a stab of disappointment. She didn't have a "scoop." Then she looked at the equipment in her car and realized she still could beat out the TV crew. She had the ability to broadcast sooner.

Suddenly the scanner came alive again with shouting. The gunman was coming out with the hostage. They were in the doorway of the house. They were on the steps. Daisy sped down the cross street. She didn't want to miss seeing the gunman. She took the corner and found at least half the road clogged with police cars. They'd kept a lane open for emergency vehicles, and Daisy told herself this was an emergency. She was relieved that she was driving a compact and could squeeze through the narrow corridor of empty roadway. A man darted from between two parked cars. Daisy slammed on the brakes the moment she saw him, but it was too late. She would never forget the look of astonishment on his face just before impact—just before he was deflected off her right front fender.

An instant later the area was swarming with police. Daisy's car door was opened and she was helped out. The minicam appeared.

Medics and police surrounded the man Daisy had hit.

Daisy tried to go to the man, but she was restrained by a policeman. "Is he all right?" she asked. "This is terrible!" She felt the tears gathering behind her eyes.

The man was on his feet, swearing at Daisy. "I'm gonna get you!" he said. "You're a marked woman. Your life is gone, sister."

"I'm sorry," Daisy said. "I didn't see you . . ."

"It wasn't your fault," the policeman told Daisy. "You were going real slow, and there was no way you could have seen him. He ran right into the side of your car. Besides, you're a hero. He let the little girl go and made a run for it, but we couldn't get near him what with all these bystanders. We might have lost him if you hadn't knocked him on his keister."

"Oh no," Daisy said. "Are you telling me that man was the gunman?"

The minicam zoomed in on Daisy.

"How does it feel to have captured Barry LeRoy, the Roach?" a woman asked.

"Well, I didn't exactly capture him," Daisy said. "I sort of inadvertently ran into him."

The minicam swung around to record the Roach, handcuffed now, being led to the paddy wagon.

The woman continued the interview. "Are you a police officer?" she asked Daisy, noting the antennae sticking out of her car like porcupine quills.

"*No!* Goodness. I'm the WZZZ traffic reporter. I was hoping for an interview. I suppose it's too late for that," Daisy said, watching the doors clang closed on the police van.

Steve Crow was on his way to the pound to get a dog when he heard the bulletin come over the radio. The Dog Lady of Snore had just run down the Roach, a major dope dealer. Steve made a U-turn and put in a call to the station.

"Who the devil sent her out on an interview?" Steve yelled into his phone.

"I did," the editor said. "I thought that's what she was supposed to do. We always use the traffic cars as mobile units."

"She bakes dog biscuits!" Steve shouted. "For crying out loud, she gives fashion reports on accident victims."

"It's the human interest angle," the editor said. "People seem to like it."

Steve slammed the phone into its cradle. He knew people liked it. In fact, he, too, found it pleasant to have the traffic report humanized. What he'd actually been thinking, but didn't dare say, was that Daisy Adams, despite her cheerful busyness and obvious competency, seemed fragile and vulnerable to him. He wanted to care for her, protect her. He definitely did not want her running around in bad neighborhoods and bagging dope dealers.

He dialed her car-phone number and clenched his teeth while he waited. One ring, two rings. "Come on, come on," he said. When she answered he didn't bother with hello. "Are you all right?" he asked.

"Yup. I'm fine."

"Is it true you ran down Barry LeRoy?"

"Sort of. He kind of bounced off my fender. It was an accident."

Steve clenched his teeth again and counted to ten. "Okay, where are you now?"

"I'm on my way to the station."

"Good. I'll meet you at the garage."

"Do you have Bob?" Daisy asked. "The editor said you went home to get Bob."

Steve smacked his forehead with the heel of his hand. "Yeah, I have Bob. We'll both meet you at the garage."

He made another U-turn. The pound was only a few miles away. He still had time to pick up a dog. It wouldn't be so bad, he told himself. A dog was man's best friend. They could go jogging together. And Bob would be waiting for him when he came home each evening. Coming home to an empty house had gotten old lately. This was going to work out fine. In fact, he couldn't imagine why he hadn't thought to get a dog sooner.

Five minutes later Steve followed a young woman in a blue kennel coat down the rows of cages, checking out the dogs. Small mutt with perky ears; greyhound rescued from a lab; mixed breed with a litter of puppies; fox terrier . . . and Bob. Steve knew him the moment he laid eyes on him. Bob was a gray and white sheepdog. Steve knew he'd be a great pet because he looked just like the nursemaid dog in Peter Pan. He was almost as wide as he was tall. He looked like a big box with hair.

"That's him," Steve said. "That's my dog."

"He's just a puppy," the girl said. "He'll be a year old next week."

"Perfect. Wrap him up." Steve looked at his watch. "I'm running a little late."

The girl opened the cage door and put a choke collar around the dog. She clicked on a leash and handed it to Steve. "There are a few forms to fill out."

The dog bounded from his cage, put his two front paws on Steve's chest, and barked.

Steve grinned at him. "He likes me," he told the kennel attendant.

He had his first doubts about Bob when he opened the car door for him and the dog barely fit through. He had more serious doubts when he slid behind the wheel and couldn't find the gearshift under Bob's tail. Bob began to pant in the close quarters. A glob of drool plopped onto Steve's shoulder. The windows fogged. Steve opened the sun roof and Bob tipped his nose up for fresh air.

"This isn't going to work," Steve said. "The car is too small." He pushed against Bob, trying to find the car phone, but Bob was sitting on it. In truth, he had no place else to sit. "Okay," Steve said, "just hang in there. I'm going to fix this. We have to make the best of it for a few miles." He turned the air-conditioning on full blast and opened the windows, deciding Bob needed a few lessons in personal hygiene.

Ten minutes later Steve and Bob were in a new-car showroom looking at Jeeps. "What about this one?" Steve said to Bob. "You like red?"

Bob wagged his tail.

"I'll take it," Steve said to the salesman. "I want to trade in that black car in the parking lot. The one with dog drool on the windshield."

The salesman blinked at the car. "You can't trade that in. It's worth at least thirty thousand dollars more than the car you're buying!"

He was right, Steve realized. The car was almost new. "Okay," he said, taking out his checkbook. "I'll pay cash for the Jeep. I'll leave the black car here and pick it up later . . . maybe tomorrow."

He called Daisy while the salesman was completing the paperwork. "I'm going to be a little late," he said. "Do you mind waiting for me?"

"No," Daisy said, "I just got here myself."

"I'm only around the corner. I'll be there in half an hour tops."

Steve drove out of the showroom humming happily. This was much better. They'd put the backseat down and Bob had lots of room to stretch out. He didn't smell any better, but he'd stopped panting and drooling. And this wasn't a woman-catcher car, Steve thought. He wouldn't have to worry about finding panties on his antenna.

His heart beat a little faster when he saw Daisy. She was wearing a black tank top and a white linen skirt that stopped an inch above her knees. "That's her," he said to Bob. "That's Daisy, possibly the future mother of my children. What do you think? Great legs, huh?"

Bob started panting again.

Steve patted him on top of his head. "I know just how you feel," he said to Bob. "I feel like panting, too, but you have to learn to control these body functions. Take my word for it . . . women don't usually like to be drooled on." He parked the car next to Daisy and went around to open the door for Bob.

Bob jumped out, happily lunged at Daisy, and pinned her to the WZZZ car, his paws planted on her chest.

Steve studied Bob's technique and wondered if it'd work for him. Bob even received a hug. Steve pulled the dog off Daisy and encouraged him to sit down. "He's a tad low on manners," Steve explained. "He's a puppy. He hasn't been to obedience school yet."

Bob's mouth fell open and his eyes widened in alarm.

"I don't think he likes the idea of obedience school," Daisy said, fondling Bob's droopy ears.

"Sure he does. Only the other day he was telling me how he wanted a chance to do some socializing."

Bob looked at Steve with his head cocked and his eyes narrowed.

"Jeez," Daisy said, "if I could put that look

into words I'd probably be embarrassed to say them."

Steve thought he was beginning to understand why Bob had been left at the pound. "He needs food. You know how it is with youngsters, if you don't keep feeding them they get cranky." He leveled a look at Bob that implied neutering might follow obedience school. The warning wasn't necessary. At the mention of the word "food" Bob snapped to attention. His mouth tipped up into a smile. His tail thumped the cement floor. His eyes brightened.

"I have just the thing," Daisy said. "A nice nutritious stir-fry dinner."

"We'll follow you home," Steve said. "I want to make sure nothing else happens to you today."

Daisy rolled her eyes. "That isn't necessary. I'll be fine. Until today I had an impeccable driving record."

"Humor me."

Steve and Bob got back into the Jeep and waited for Daisy. A moment later she drove by and waved to them. The car was yellow and maroon, or at least might have been yellow and maroon when it was new. Steve could barely see for the exhaust. New had been a lot of years ago. Valves clattered, the fan belt whistled, the muffler rattled, and the beast left a trail of oil that reminded Steve of Hansel and Gretel's bread crumbs.

Forty-five minutes later Daisy had a mound of food on her chopping block and was waiting for her electric wok to heat up. "It's my mom's," she said to Steve. "She sent over a box full of pots and pans, hoping Kevin wouldn't starve to death before they returned from Texas."

Kevin was forlornly staring into an empty bag of chips. "Bob ate all my chips."

"He's a puppy," Steve said, throwing a black look at Bob.

Daisy added oil to the wok. "I hope he hasn't ruined his appetite."

Kevin looked at Bob sprawled across the kitchen floor. "I don't think this house is big enough for the two of us. He's a nice dog, Steve, but he's moving in on my territory."

Steve could appreciate Kevin's point of view. Bob was getting more than his share of attention from Daisy. He was getting hugs and kisses and tasty morsels of food. When they got home tonight, Steve was going to have a long talk with Bob. He was going to tell him about hogging the chips and moving in on a budding relationship.

Daisy dumped the meat and vegetables into the wok and stirred.

Bob was on his feet beside her. His tail was swishing back and forth, his ears were perked up, his mouth was open in joyous expectation.

"He sure gets excited about food," Daisy said.

"So do I," Kevin told her. "I get excited about food. Doesn't anyone want to feed me?"

"We're going out to eat," Steve said. "I was supposed to bring the people food, but things got sort of hectic, and I didn't get a chance to shop."

Daisy scooped the stir fry into a heavy ceramic bowl, blew on it, and when it was cool, she said to Bob, "Bon appétit." She set the bowl on the floor.

Bob made a few loud grunting, slurping, snorting noises, and the food was gone. He sat back and studied the bowl, as if more food might suddenly appear. He had a slim scrap of sautéed pepper stuck in his chin whiskers. Steve thought Kevin looked like he was thinking about eating it, but Bob sniffed, located the pepper slice with his tongue, and swallowed it before Kevin had a chance to snatch it away.

Daisy still had the fork in her hand. "I thought you said this dog was finicky."

"Probably he draws the line at table legs," Kevin said.

Steve picked the bowl up off the floor. It was licked so clean it looked like it had just come out of the dishwasher. "I guess my food isn't as good as your food."

Daisy smiled. "This is one recipe that will definitely get included in my next book."

Steve put a friendly arm around Daisy. "Now for my part of the bargain. I'm going to take you guys to a first-class restaurant."

"Excellent," Kevin said, already at the door. "Do I get to ride in the car from hell?"

"Afraid not. I don't have the car from hell today. Today I have the Jeep from Chrysler," Steve said.

"That's okay," Kevin said. "Jeeps are cool."

Daisy slung her purse over her shoulder. "What'll we do about Bob?"

The question took Steve by surprise. He wasn't used to worrying about dogs. "Could we leave him in your backyard?"

"Fang ate a hole through my privacy fence. Bob would be able to escape. I suppose we could leave him in the house, though."

"You be a good dog," Steve told Bob. "Don't do anything rude in the house, and I'll take you for a walk when we come back."

Daisy closed and locked the door and was halfway to the car when an unearthly sound stopped her in her tracks. "My Lord, what *is* that?"

Everyone listened. The pitch rose. Bob was howling for all he was worth.

"He's lonely," Daisy said, returning to the house. "We'll have to take him with us." She unlocked the door and snapped Bob's leash on his choke collar. "We can go to one of those fast-food drive-throughs. Then we won't have to leave Bob home alone."

Bob galloped to the car and jumped onto the backseat beside Kevin.

When everyone ordered at the drive-through, Bob got two burgers and a vanilla shake. He was vastly subdued on the way home, and by the time Daisy and Steve had cleaned the kitchen and were ready to settle themselves in front of the TV to hear the eleven o'clock news, Bob was sound asleep on the couch.

Steve liked Bob a lot when he was sleeping. Not only was Bob adorable, but he was also taking up most of the couch, making it necessary for everyone else to sit pressed together, squeezed into the remaining few inches. Since Kevin had gone to his room to avoid drying dishes, the squeezing was left to Steve and Daisy. Steve sat down and waited for Daisy to sit beside him.

She stood with hands on hips, surveying the space left available to her. All right! This was her chance to snuggle next to Steve Crow. She felt giddy with anticipation, but she didn't want to seem too eager, so she pretended there wasn't enough room for her. "Your dog is a couch hog." God bless him.

"I could move him," Steve offered. He didn't mean it, of course. He wouldn't move that dog if the house was on fire. Good old Bob had finally done something right.

"He looks so comfy."

As if on cue Bob rolled over, feet in the air, looking twice as comfy as before.

"That settles it," Daisy said, wedging herself next to Steve. "He's really a sweetie-pie."

Steve put his arm around her, and everywhere their bodies met he felt warmth. It crept through his shirt and the fabric of his gray slacks and heated his blood. He realized it had been a long time since he'd been this easily aroused. Probably not since ninth grade when he'd felt a girl's breast for the first time. Mary Lou Resnick, he thought fondly. He could still remember the look in her eyes. At the time he'd thought it was unbridled passion; now he recognized it as pure terror.

Daisy was experiencing a lot of both. The touch of his hand at her shoulder sent a shock of desire to the pit of her stomach. The intensity of the desire prompted a wave of apprehension. If she had any sense, she'd be sitting in the club chair on the other side of the room, she thought. He was going to kiss her, and she was going to respond by tearing his clothes off and embarrassing herself. She turned toward him and heard him suck in his breath when her breast flattened against the wall of his chest. "Oops," she said, "maybe we're sitting too close."

His answer was a kiss that made her toes curl.

As far as he was concerned they weren't nearly close enough. He kissed her again and wondered what it was about this woman that had him constantly wanting. Just the thought of her drove all logic from his mind. He'd adopted a dog because of her! He'd bought a new car. Since she'd walked into his office yesterday, he'd instantly turned into a scheming lech. And if all that wasn't bad enough, he was falling in love with her. Must be a mid-life crisis, he decided, although thirty-two seemed a little young. He felt her move against him and thought was pushed aside.

They would never have heard Kevin if it hadn't been for his size-fourteen feet. He thundered down the stairs with the speed he usually reserved for locating a refrigerator. "Hey, you guys, do you have the TV on? Daisy made the news!"

Daisy sat up and blinked, embarrassed. She'd forgotten about Kevin being in the house. She made a fast check of her clothes and was relieved to find them all in order. "What do you mean, I made the news?"

"Look," Kevin said, sitting in front of the television, "it's you!"

The camera focused on Daisy being interviewed by the woman reporter and then panned to the gunman, swearing and threatening to get even.

Steve was stunned. "He threatened you!"

"He got excited. He didn't mean it," Daisy said.

"How do you know? How can you be sure?"

"For goodness sake, he doesn't even know me."

"He does now," Steve said. "You've just been on national television."

"He's been arrested," Daisy insisted. "He's locked up. He couldn't hurt me even if he wanted to."

"That guy is one of the biggest dope dealers in Washington. He was out on bail before you even arrived home tonight. And he has friends. Lots of ugly friends."

"I'll be careful. I'll be especially careful if I see any ugly people who look like dope dealers."

"Damn right you'll be careful. You'll stay here in this house until that guy comes to trial. I'll hire a bodyguard, I'll buy an attack dog, I'll install an alarm system."

Daisy put her hand to his forehead. The kiss had gotten pretty hot, but she didn't think it was enough to make him delirious. "Maybe you need some fresh air."

"I don't need fresh air. I need peace of mind. I'm not going to have you cruising the city in the newscar when some maniacal dope dealer is out to get you."

Daisy narrowed her eyes at him. "Exactly what are you saying?"

"I'm saying you're fired. You're grounded. You're confined to quarters."

"You can't do that to me! I need the money, and I like the job. I was beginning to get good at it."

"I'll *give* you the money. I'll pay you to stay home."

"It's not the same."

"Don't be an idiot," Kevin said. "Take the money."

Four

Daisy pulled into the Shulster Building underground garage and was relieved to find the newscar still in its parking space. Steve had left in a huff last night. Actually, she'd sort of kicked him out. He'd insisted she didn't have a job, and she'd threatened a lawsuit. She was sure she'd been discriminated against, but she wasn't sure exactly how. This morning she'd woken filled with resolve to do the traffic report. She figured she was on the winning side. If Steve knew anyone else who could do the traffic report, he would never have given the job to her in the first place.

Her optimism vanished when she saw him lounging against his Jeep four cars down. He had his arms loosely crossed over his chest, his mouth was firm and unsmiling, his eyes were dark and brooding. If she'd run across him looking like this three days ago, she'd have panicked. Today she stiffened her spine, tipped her nose up a fraction of an inch, and told herself he was a man like any other man. She knew it wasn't completely true. But for her purposes this morning she preferred to delude herself into thinking he was average and manageable.

She parked her car and left it unlocked. The locks were rusted out, and besides, as far as she was concerned, if anyone was dumb enough to steal her wreck, then he deserved to have to drive it. She walked over to Steve and stood toe to toe with him. "Well?" she said.

"If I wasn't so damned frustrated, I'd probably admire your nerve."

"I'll be fine."

"I hate to hear you say that!" He ran his hand through his hair. "What am I supposed to do with all my macho protective instincts? Why are you making my life so difficult?"

"Gosh, I never thought of it in those terms."

"Well, think about it." He pulled her to him and kissed her. The kiss deepened, his hands slid the length of her spine and crushed her to him.

Daisy's stomach tumbled. It was difficult to maintain her delusions when reality pressed hard against her stomach. Steve Crow was definitely more man than most in several ways. One was much more noticeable than the others.

The kiss was disturbed by the pager on his belt. He pushed her away and swore softly. "I have a meeting."

"I promise to be careful."

"Good. As an added precaution I'm hiring a guard to ride with you."

"What?"

"The agency is sending three people. You can interview them and take your pick. They're to meet you at the park in two hours." Before she could answer he turned and strode away.

"I don't want a guard!" she shouted, but he was gone.

At one o'clock he called on the car phone. "How's everything going?"

"Couldn't be better."

"Do you have a guard with you?"

"Yup."

"Good. I'll meet both of you at the garage tonight. I want to make the terms of the job clear to him."

Daisy gave her last report at three fifty-five and the newscar reached the garage ten minutes later. Steve was waiting for her. Daisy got out and waved to him, and an old lady followed her. She had steel-gray hair curled neat and tight against her skull. She was shorter than Daisy and as slim, but not so curvy, Steve reflected. She wore clean white tennis shoes and carried a big patent-leather purse with a gold snap top. There wasn't anyone else in the newscar.

"What happened to the guard?" Steve asked.

"I didn't feel comfortable with any of them,"

Daisy told him. "So I got my own guard. I hope that's okay."

The old lady held out her hand. "Elsie Hawkins. Rough and Ready Security Guard Service. Class of ninety-one."

Steve felt his mouth drop open. He shifted his weight and looked at both women, trying to determine if this was a joke. "I've never heard of Rough and Ready Security Guard Service."

"It was one of them mail-order courses," Elsie said. "But it's legit. I got a certificate and everything. I did it while I was on the mend in the nursing home."

"You're not serious."

"Damn serious," Elsie said.

"You graduated from guard school while you were in a nursing home?"

"Yup. I broke my hip skiing in Vermont and they had to put one of them steel contraptions in, so I took this correspondence course to keep from going nuts in rehab." She lifted her right leg. "See? It's almost as good as new. Except of course I have to be careful about going out in an electrical storm with all these metal parts."

Steve searched for words but couldn't find any.

"That's a joke," Elsie said. She shook her head at Daisy. "He's a looker, but he's not too bright."

"Excuse us," Steve said to Elsie, pulling Daisy by the arm. "I'd like to talk to Miss Adams in private a moment." He walked Daisy five cars down and backed her against a van.

"What's going on. What's with the squirrelly old lady?"

"She's not squirrelly. She's perfectly capable. And she really did graduate from the Rough and Ready Guard School. I saw her certificate. We had a nice ceremony for her at the rehabilitation center."

Steve pulled Daisy back to Elsie Hawkins. "I'm sorry, Miss Hawkins, but I don't think this is going to work. Miss Adams's life is in danger, and I need a real guard."

"Stop the presses," Daisy said. "Elsie *is* a real guard, and she's the one I chose." She thumped herself on the chest. "I'm the one who has to spend all day with this guard person." Another thump. "I'm the one who should be concerned about her qualifications." She tossed her hair over her shoulder with a snap of her head. "I'm the one who is ultimately responsible for my personal safety. So I should have the last word in picking out my guard. And another thing. It would be hypocritical of me to discriminate against the elderly."

"I'm the one paying the bill. And I'm the one losing sleep over it," Steve said.

Elsie made a disgusted sound with her tongue. "Well, make up your minds if you want me. This isn't the only security-guard job in town, you know. And I got better things to do than to stand here and watch you two argue. I gotta be home by six to see a TV show about blood pressure."

Steve smacked his forehead with the heel of

his hand. "I don't believe this. This is insane." He looked at Daisy. "What is this woman going to do if someone threatens you?"

Elsie pulled a .45 magnum long-barrel out of her pocketbook and leveled it at Steve's zipper. "I'd shoot him in the privates. Some people aim for the heart, some people like to gut-shoot a man, but I always aim for the privates. Word gets around when you shoot off a man's privates. People get to be real careful of you. Yessir, I could blow a hole in you the size of a potato with this baby."

"Holy cow!" Steve pushed Daisy behind a car. "Where'd you get that bazooka? And what are you doing carrying it around in your pocketbook?"

Elsie put the gun back in her purse and closed it with a firm snap. "Got it at a yard sale in the District," Elsie said. "A woman's got to protect herself. I'm an old lady, you know. It isn't like I could give some pervert a karate chop."

"It isn't loaded, is it?"

"Of course it's loaded, but you don't have to worry. I know what I'm doing. The safety's on. You sure are a jumpy one," she said to Steve.

"You have a license to carry a concealed weapon?"

"People keep asking me that. One of these days I'm going to have to look into it," Elsie said.

Steve loosened his tie and popped the top button on his shirt. "I need a drink. Something cold that's going to make me numb."

"Drinking rots your liver," Elsie told him.

"And an ounce of alcohol kills a thousand brain cells."

Steve thought it was pretty clear Elsie didn't think he could afford to lose that many brain cells.

"I gotta roll," Elsie said. "I'll be back tomorrow." She climbed into a blue and white 1957 Cadillac and rumbled away with a V-8 engine and dual exhaust system that sounded like distant thunder.

"I'll follow you home," Steve said to Daisy. "How about discussing this over dinner."

"Sounds great, but I have to work at the nursing home tonight." She looked at her watch. "I better get going or I'll be late."

"How about after work? A late dinner?"

She chewed on her lower lip. It was tempting, but she was behind on her dissertation schedule. "Can't. I have a ton of reading to do for school."

His life wasn't going well, Steve decided. Everything used to be so smooth. Women never said no, old ladies used to think he was bright, people he employed followed instructions. At least he had a dog. The thought lifted his spirits. He'd go home, take Bob out for a burger, and then they'd go run a couple fast miles together. Afterward they could watch television and maybe put a frozen pie in the oven for dessert. Pretty damn domestic, he thought to himself. He'd turned into a regular family man. A Jeep, a dog, and a frozen pie. Life didn't get much better than that. Not tonight anyway.

When Steve got home there were seven notes tacked to his apartment door about Bob's howling and an eviction notice from the superintendent stating he'd violated the no-pet rule of the apartment building. When Steve opened the door, Bob rushed out to the elevator. Steve pushed the emergency express button, but they only made it to the second floor before Bob humiliated himself. They continued on down to the basement parking garage where they quickly exited the elevator. Steve pushed the elevator button for the penthouse, and then he and Bob went out in search of a realtor.

"Don't worry about it," Steve said to Bob. "It wasn't your fault. You did the best you could. I guess a dog doesn't belong in an apartment." Bob looked depressed, so Steve patted his head. "We're going to buy you a nice house. One with a big fenced-in yard." A house that was closer to Daisy, Steve thought. A house that had enough room for a few dozen kids— just in case.

Bob woofed and wagged his tail.

Two hours later Steve and Bob had a house to live in. The owners had already moved out, so Steve and Bob could rent the house until closing. It was amazing what you could do when you were willing to pay top dollar and didn't need financing, Steve thought grimly. His bank account was dwindling. He hadn't realized a dog could be such an expense.

When they returned to the apartment building they took the stairs. Steve put the pie in the oven and started packing essentials. To-morrow he'd call a mover. By tomorrow night he'd have his own tomato bush, a cozy fire-place, a gas grill in his backyard. Until recently he'd thought he hated all those things. He told himself he was buying them for Bob, but oddly enough, deep down inside, he was looking for-ward to watching his tomato bush grow.

Steve and Bob met Daisy in the garage the following morning. Daisy was wearing a khaki jacket, orange T-shirt, and khaki shorts that looked like a skirt except they had cuffs. She had a Styrofoam cup of coffee in her hand and dark circles under her eyes.

"What's Bob doing here?" she asked.

"He wanted to see where I work."

Daisy nodded sleepily, as if it were perfectly normal for a dog to go to work.

"Have a tough night?" Steve asked.

"I got home late from the rehab center, and then I had all this reading to do." She yawned and sighed. "Kevin tried to do the papers for me, but he delivered some of them to the wrong people, so I had to go out and fix things."

"I thought you were going to give up the paper route?"

"I told them I'd finish out the week."

Tomorrow he'd help her with the paper route, he decided. His new house was only half a mile away from her town house. He'd get up early and walk around with her, and then they could have breakfast together in his cozy breakfast nook that overlooked his tomato bush.

Elsie pulled up in the Caddie. She slammed the door and locked it and marched over to them. She was wearing a purple flowered dress with a little lace collar, and she was carrying the big black handbag. "Morning." She looked more closely at Daisy. "You look like the devil."

"I was up late last night. Then things got kind of rushed this morning because I had to squeeze grocery shopping in between my other jobs." She gave an enormous yawn and sighed. "I'll be okay once I get on the road. I'm used to being tired."

"Maybe Elsie should drive today," Steve said. He gave Elsie a twenty-dollar bill. "Take the portable scanner and go somewhere for breakfast."

"She's overcommitted," Elsie said. "She's headed for burnout. If she don't watch her step, she's gonna end up someplace where they feed you strained peas and make you sleep in a rubber room."

Steve scrutinized Daisy. She looked tired but she didn't look ready for the rubber room. He wasn't so sure about himself and Elsie. He could see blue sky lurking beyond the open garage door. Inside the dark garage it was cool, but the air was already heating up outside. In another hour the cement pavement would be shimmering. In another hour he'd be on the air-conditioned broadcast floor and Daisy would be cruising south on the beltway through Maryland. He didn't like the arrangements. He wanted to be with Daisy. He reached out, touched a silky curl, and let it wrap around his finger. "I think I'll carve an hour out of my schedule today so we can have lunch together. I'll get some potato salad and fried chicken and we can have a picnic."

He arrived at Belle Haven at twelve-fifteen with a packing crate filled with food and the quilt from his bed draped over his arm. Bob bounced around beside him, following close on his heels, never taking his eyes off the food box. They spread the quilt under a tree not far from the car, took the portable scanner, and set out the lunch.

Elsie looked at the quilt and shook her head. "Once I get down on that thing it's gonna take a forklift to get me up. I can do most anything with this hip except picnic. If it's all the same to you, I'll take my food back to the car."

Steve gave Bob a bag full of burgers and a vanilla milk shake. "Don't eat the carton," he told the dog. "Last time you ate the carton and it made you sick."

Daisy took some fried chicken and fruit salad. "This is lovely. You're a good person."

"I was hoping you'd notice."

She smiled at him. He had ulterior motives. How nice.

"I have some big news," he said. "I bought a house last night." He took a napkin and wiped milk shake off Bob's face fur. "It's a terrific house. It has a fenced-in backyard for Bob and little print wallpaper in the dining room. Actually, I don't know if I like the wallpaper, but the realtor said it was Williamsburg and very classy. Maybe you could take a look at it and let me know what you think. I'm not much of a judge when it comes to wallpaper."

And while she was there she could also look at the bedrooms—especially the one with his big queen-size bed.

Bob had finished his burgers and was inching his way over to the chicken.

"You can't have chicken," Steve told him. "It has bones in it and you're not supposed to have bones raw or cooked." Steve dumped a glob of potato salad on a paper plate, added a deviled egg and a biscuit, and fed it to Bob. "Save some room for dessert," he told him. "I bought a cheesecake."

Daisy slanted a look at Bob. "He always eats like this? What did he eat for breakfast?"

"We didn't have much time this morning. We were up late last night packing. We stopped on the way in to work and got coffee and doughnuts."

"You fed him coffee and doughnuts for breakfast?"

"I made sure the coffee was cool. Yesterday was better. Yesterday we had orange juice and eggs and whole wheat toast."

"Doesn't he ever eat dog food?"

"I bought some for him but he didn't like it."

Daisy ate half of a melon ball. "You ever have a dog when you were a kid?"

He shook his head. "Nope. I never had a pet of any kind until Bob. We lived in a high-rise in Houston for most of my childhood. Very posh. My dad is a minor oil tycoon. He and my mom do lots of traveling. They were never very interested in the hearth-and-home stuff. Home was a place to entertain business associates."

"You probably had servants."

"Mmmm." He gnawed on a chicken leg and tossed it into the cardboard bucket. He glanced at Daisy and thought she looked a little wistful."

"Must have been nice."

He shrugged. "It was right for my mom and dad. They both came from very poor beginnings. When the oil money started coming in they went uptown. My grandfather Crow was the only member of the family who stayed on the land. I spent a summer with him once and hated it. I must have been nine or ten. I look back on it now and think it might have been the best summer I ever had."

Daisy curled her legs under her and picked at a biscuit. "What made you change your mind after all those years?"

"I don't know. Gut feeling. My grandfather Crow lived on a flat piece of cracked red dirt. The house was a small wooden thing patched together with pieces of jerry can and chinked with sun-dried mud. He swept the inside with a broom. He didn't have a vacuum cleaner. He had electricity but he only used it in the winter to run the heater. No electric lights. He said they made the life cycle unnatural. He said when the sun went down a body was supposed to look at the stars for a while and go to sleep. And if you couldn't fall asleep right off, you hadn't worked hard enough that day." His grin was lopsided, self-deprecating. "This philosophy went over big with a ten-year-old who'd never known a day without servants. I didn't know how to pour my own milk on my cereal. And I thought watching television was an essential body function—eating, sleeping, watching television. Grandpa Crow had a garden behind his house that he worked on every day. He had to keep whacking at the red dirt to keep it from baking hard and dry around his plants. He had a goat and a flock of scrawny chickens. He had an old Ford pickup that was in worse shape than your klunker, and every Saturday we'd go into town for some canned food and mail and Grandpa'd get a bottle of whiskey. When he was alone I think he might have been drunk a lot of the time, but when I was there he'd just sip at the whiskey and get more talkative." The grin broadened. "By normal standards more talkative wasn't exactly chatty. Grandpa Crow was a man of few words."

"Is he still living on his land?"

"Yeah. I went to see him two years ago. He'd moved into a trailer. Very spiffy, but he still wasn't using lights. At least that's what he said, but I think when no one's around he pulls out a television and makes microwave popcorn."

"How about you? Do you have servants now?"

"Someone comes in to clean." He polished off another chicken leg. "I learned how to pour my own milk when I was in college, so I was able to do away with the butler and the cook and the manservant."

"Do you miss them?"

"Sometimes the cook. Once in a while the manservant. Never the butler."

Daisy gave him a long look. "Are you at all like your grandfather?"

"Not much. I'm also not much like my parents. Lately I'm not even like myself."

"Are you having an identity crisis?"

"I think I'm in a period of transition."

"Ah-hah."

Steve sighed. She was so incredibly pretty, sitting there with her feet tucked up like a cat and her blond hair dappled in sunlight. Very feminine. He reconsidered the word. "Feminine" didn't feel exactly right. "Womanly" was better. There was a ripeness to her, a lushness of personality. She didn't whine or flirt or make excuses. She went about the business of living with open exuberance. In an odd way she reminded him of his grandfather. His grandfather Crow was much more taciturn, but there was depth to him, and there was depth to Daisy.

In the beginning Steve had felt the pull of her blue eyes and soft curves, and instantly falling in love with her had been half serious, half folly—a private joke on himself that held an element of truth. This morning he woke up and realized that he wasn't just enamored—he liked her. Really liked her. She was brave and bright and honest. And there was a lot of passion bubbling below the surface. He suspected she hadn't fully tapped into it yet. There was a breathless element to her kisses. It was as if she were always astonished, always pleasantly surprised by the chemistry that existed between them. He understood that astonishment. He felt it too.

"Oh my Lord," Daisy said, jumping to her feet. "Look at the time!" She dashed to the car, stuffed the plug in her ear, and grabbed the two-way.

She came back and dropped onto the quilt. "Just made it. I put the plug in my ear when the cue came up." She looked guilty. "I gave the same report as last time. I'm probably not supposed to admit that to my boss."

"It'll cost you. I might fire you if you don't agree to help me figure out the gas grill tonight."

"Job harassment."

"Absolutely."

"I'm not worried. You've tried to fire me before."

"Does that mean you won't help me with the grill?"

"Of course I'll help you with the grill." She stretched out on her stomach with her head resting on her arm. "After all, what are friends for?"

"Is that what we are? Friends?"

She felt heat flood to her cheeks. "I don't know what we are. Friends seems like a good place to start."

He watched her eyelids drift closed and studied the fringe of blond lash that had received a cursory swipe with the mascara wand. Her breathing slowed, her mouth softened. She was asleep. He glanced at his watch. If he canceled the rest of his day, he could do the traffic reports and let her sleep. He mentally reviewed his agenda and grunted. There'd be hell to pay if he canceled his afternoon.

He packed up what remained of the food and clicked the leash on Bob. He went to Elsie and spoke quietly so he wouldn't wake Daisy. "I have to get back to the station. Let her sleep as long as possible. She has to broadcast another traffic report in ten minutes."

"She's one of them givers," Elsie said. "Never says no to anybody, but there's only so much responsibility a person can take on."

Steve was on the beltway when the next traffic report cued in.

"Hello, hello?" An elderly voice came over the airwaves. "I don't know if I'm working this dang thing right, but if you can hear me I'm gonna give a traffic report. This is Elsie Hawkins and I'm only gonna tell you all this stuff once so you better listen up . . ."

Four days ago he would have been emptying the aspirin bottle, Steve thought. But here he was smiling at Elsie Hawkins. He and a thousand other listeners. Eventually Frank would get his cast cut off and he'd be back doing traffic in his clipped, no-nonsense manner. In the meantime, it was summer, and the listening audience was in a more relaxed frame of mind. Everyone seemed to be enjoying the off-beat reports.

Bob was sitting next to him with the seat belt clipped around his shoulders and his head out the window. His ears were flapping in the wind and his tongue flopped out of the side of his mouth. His expression was blissful.

Steve looked at him and woofed, but Bob just kept smiling.

Five

Steve slouched behind the wheel and closed his eyes as traffic momentarily stopped. Now he remembered why he'd originally decided to live in the high rise. It was five blocks from the station and there was never any traffic. He hated sitting in traffic. Ten minutes ago he'd punched the radio off and put a tape into the deck because he couldn't stand hearing another depressing traffic report. There was a disabled car stuck in an intersection up ahead, and the resulting backup now stretched three miles. It would probably get worse before it got better. Not even a tow truck could cut through gridlock. A tow truck had to inch along just like everybody else.

Daisy was probably somewhere in front of him in this mess, Steve thought. He'd been delayed in a meeting, and she'd been unable to wait. Something about books due at the library and Kevin needing a ride to a friend's house. Daisy didn't have many minutes to spare.

He glanced in the rearview mirror at Bob. Bob was sound asleep in the back, his nose stuffed up against the air-conditioning vent. Tough life.

Steve drummed his fingers on the steering wheel, letting the car creep forward. He couldn't wait to get a look at the idiot causing this disaster. If it turned out to be some fool who ran out of gas, he'd choke him with his bare hands. He heard the *whup, whup, whup* of chopper blades and looked up to see the WZZZ helicopter pass overhead. Pride shot through him, followed by frustration. WZZZ was going to tell him there was traffic on Braddock Road. No kidding! At least he was getting closer to the source of the problem. Cars were feeding into a single lane and orange lights flashed in the distance, signalling that a tow truck was on the scene. When he was three cars back from the flashing lights, traffic came to another standstill. He stuck his head out in time to hear a motor churn and catch. A hood was slammed down while someone revved the disabled car engine. A thick cloud of black exhaust billowed over the tow truck and drifted back to Steve, temporarily obscuring his view. When the cloud lifted he could see the car that had caused the traffic jam pull ahead and proceed down the road without the aid of a tow truck. The car was old. It was covered with rust and had a coat-hanger antenna. The rear bumper dipped on the right side where it had been snagged by another car eons ago. The paint was faded but probably had been maroon and yellow. There was only one car like it in Northern Virginia—possibly in the world. It belonged to Daisy.

"We have to get her out of that car," Steve said to Bob. "It's a health hazard. And it's a threat to my sanity."

Bob looked up from the backseat.

"I have a plan," Steve told him. "I'm not going to tell you about it because it's dastardly and you're obviously a dog of high moral fiber."

Daisy zoomed into Steve's driveway at seven o'clock and hit the ground running. "Sorry I'm late!" she said to Steve, adjusting the pink T-shirt she'd thrown on just five minutes earlier. A small swath of flesh was exposed between shorts and shirt and no amount of tugging would fill in the gap. "Damn," she said, "it must have shrunk in the dryer."

Steve took in the cut-off denim shorts and slightly-too-small shirt and thought they looked perfect. He was highly in favor of exposing Daisy's flesh. "You're not late. And I needed some time to unpack a few things and organize the kitchen. Moving is hell, even when you hire a great company that's supposed to do it all for you in one fell swoop."

Daisy looked at the brick colonial and smiled in approval. It was only a few years old and had been nicely landscaped. There was about a quarter of an acre and the backyard was fenced. If he'd had a wife and three kids, it would have been the ideal house. As it was, it seemed a tad large for a bachelor. Of course there was Bob to help fill it. "It's nice," she said. "I've always liked a traditional colonial."

He turned to lead her through the house, and she did a fast body assessment, admiring slim hips and a perfect backside. He wore khaki shorts with a black T-shirt that showed off corded forearms and well-developed biceps. His legs had lots of muscle definition in the quads and calves. He hadn't gotten that kind of body from sitting behind a desk all day, and she wondered how he managed to keep in such good shape. Most of the men she knew were starting to soften in the middle. Even the tennis players and spa-goers seemed to lose tone as they climbed the corporate ladder.

He stopped at the kitchen and took a platter of raw hamburger patties from the refrigerator. "What can I get you to drink? Beer, wine, soda?"

"Soda."

He gave her a root beer, a bag of chips, and two bowls of salsa to carry outside.

"Two bowls of salsa?" she asked.

"One for Bob. I hate when he dips his chips in mine."

The phone rang and Steve answered it in the kitchen. He hung up a few minutes later, frowning. "That was security at the station. They caught someone tinkering with the newscar. The guy pulled a gun on the guard who found him and got away."

"My Lord, maybe the Roach really *is* out to get me!"

"Let's not panic. We don't know for sure. Didn't fit the Roach's description."

"Could be one of his friends."

"Could be."

"Was there any damage to the car?"

"Nothing noticeable." That was a lie. The man had written "Death to the Dog Lady" in spray paint on the side of the car.

"Well, that's a relief. And I'm glad you're taking this so calmly." She pushed the back door open and carried the chips outside. "I guess I overreacted. Not much we can do about it anyway, is there?"

"We can take you out of the traffic car."

Daisy put the chips and salsa on the picnic table. "Haven't we had this discussion before?"

"Last time we yelled at each other. This time we need to talk."

"Okay. That sounds fair. Go ahead and talk." She straddled a picnic bench and opened the bag of chips. "Put the hamburgers on the grill first. I'm starved, and Bob looks desperate."

"There's a remote possibility that this guy meant to harm you. I think we need to take precautions against that."

"We did take precautions. We hired Elsie."

Steve groaned.

"Well, okay, so she's not some big macho guard, but she's very dedicated . . . and your hamburgers are on fire."

Steve smacked at them with the spatula, but they kept burning.

"Must be your flame is too high," Daisy said.

He fidgeted with a few knobs and the flames subsided. "I've never barbecued before," he said, examining the charred hamburgers. "You think these are too done?" He slid a spatula under one and it crumbled and fell into the fire. The next one slipped off the spatula and fell onto the grass and Bob ate it. The third one made it to a bun, but nobody wanted to eat it—not even Bob.

"I don't think I have the knack for barbecue-ing," Steve said. "Maybe I'm not cut out for this suburban stuff."

Daisy patted his hand. "Of course you are. We'll try it again tomorrow. Where's your pea-nut butter?"

An hour later they were stuffed with peanut butter sandwiches and were making their way through a quart of chocolate-chip ice cream. It was eighty-seven degrees outside, but they'd built a fire in the fireplace and were sitting in front of it, eating from the ice-cream carton. They sat on the floor with their backs to the couch because Bob had claimed the couch first and was now stretched the length of it. At least that's the excuse they made for sitting on the floor. The truth is the floor seemed less threatening. There were no cush-ions to mark boundaries on the floor. They could sit side by side and the invasion of personal body space wasn't so noticeable.

Daisy stole a glance at him as he dipped his

spoon into the ice cream, then handed the carton to her. The sun was setting, and they hadn't bothered to turn on the lights. His face was lit by the fire and seemed extraordinarily sexy. His eyes were shadowed, the line of his mouth drawn firm as he followed secret thoughts, and she found she was still a little frightened of him when he looked like this. Or maybe it was the proximity that was frightening. They were so close that if she leaned toward him ever so slightly, they'd be touching. It was a tantalizing thought, and it sent a dark sort of thrill racing through her stomach.

"Last scoop of ice cream," Daisy said. "You want it?"

"Wouldn't touch it. You eat the last scoop of ice cream and you're destined to become an old maid. My aunt Zena told me that."

Daisy ate the last scoop and set the carton aside. "I don't have an aunt Zena so it doesn't count for me."

"It counts for everyone. You're in big trouble."

"I like to live dangerously. I take my chances."

His eyes shifted to her mouth and she could feel desire growing between them. It felt like a thunderstorm gathering on the horizon. He was going to kiss her and this time there'd be nothing to stop the kiss from turning into something much more serious. No Kevin in the next room, no pager to remind him of a meeting. She'd have to rely on her self-control . . . not something she could count on in this instance, she decided. She took a moment to debate the issue and reached the conclusion that sleeping with Steve Crow wouldn't be in her best interest. She didn't have the personality to dally, and Steve Crow looked like a dallier. More important, she didn't have the time to devote to a romance. That last thought prompted an unconscious sigh of regret.

"I don't like the sound of that sigh," Steve said.

"I should be going home. I have studying to do."

He slid his arm around her shoulders and playfully tugged on a curl. "What about living dangerously? What about taking chances?"

"I think I've tested the fates enough for one night."

His hand curled around her neck and heat flooded through her as he drew her closer. "Don't you want to hear what Aunt Zena has to say about missed opportunities?"

"You probably don't even have an Aunt Zena."

"That's not the point," he whispered into her hair.

She felt him kiss her just below her ear, felt his lips working their way around to her mouth, felt his hand slide under the too-short shirt. She gave herself one last warning. This is a mistake, she told herself. Their relationship would be irrevocably changed if they made love. Maybe not in his eyes, but certainly in hers. She couldn't treat it lightly. It would bring a whole new set of responsibilities with it, and she already had more responsibility than she could handle. She was drowning in responsibility. And even worse would be the emotional investment. She was already halfway in love with him. He was caring and generous and fun. He could be oddly vulnerable without ever seeming insecure. And she admired his balance. He had his ducks in a row while she felt as if hers were all quacking for attention at once. Her clutch of ducks had gotten unwieldy and a little frantic. She'd never thought of herself as being unstable, but she was afraid of going on emotional overload if she allowed herself to fall more deeply in love.

Her arguments may have been valid, but they didn't amount to a damn when he claimed her mouth. Her aspirations, responsibilities, carefully thought through plans for the future, and her fears skittered off as passion poured through her. She responded to his kiss with a kiss of her own that told him everything he needed to know. She wanted to be loved. She was hungry for it. In fact, she was more than hungry; she was starved.

She was a woman too long deprived of purely selfish pleasures, and now she kissed him with wanton abandon, inviting the most intimate of caresses. His fingertips enflamed where they touched—and she encouraged them to touch her everywhere. She tore at her clothes, needing to be free of them. There was no modesty to this passion. This passion was voracious, all-consuming, and starkly honest.

His was no less. He was wild with wanting her, greedy to know her every erotic secret, obsessed with her pleasure, letting her pleasure fuel his own. He reveled in the knowledge that he could drive her to fever-pitch—and he burned right along with her.

She opened to him, begging, whimpering, and finally demanding, desperate for fulfillment. When it came it was cataclysmic.

They lay together for a while afterward, sweat-slicked and replete.

He trailed his fingertips across her temple, stroking the hair back from her face. He didn't speak because he wasn't sure he could trust his voice. Passion had been temporarily quenched, and had been replaced by tender possession so strong it took his breath away.

She was the first to stir, pulling her head back so she could see his eyes. She was embarrassed in the aftermath of the storm. "I think I got carried away," she said.

His voice was softly reverent. "Lady, carried away doesn't begin to say it." He rolled to his side and kissed her. "I hope your intentions are honorable."

"Honorable?"

"I'm not easy, you know. I have standards. I expect you to make an honest man of me. Especially after we did all this in front of Bob."

"I don't think you have to worry about Bob. I'm not sure he's breathing. Maybe you should hold a mirror under his nose."

His hand slid down to cup a breast. "My reputation is at stake."

"Just exactly what is it you expect me to do?"

"Marry me, of course."

Daisy giggled. "Of course."

"You're not taking me seriously."

He was lying sprawled on his back, and he seemed perfectly comfortable while Daisy felt more self-conscious with each passing second. She felt physically and mentally naked, and she wasn't used to either. She'd practically attacked him. Granted there'd been sexual tension crackling between them since day one, but until this evening she'd managed to be civil about it. Until this evening she'd managed to hide her randiness, or at least to conceal it a little. Now he knew she was deprived and desperate. Or maybe he thought she was like this with everyone! She didn't know which would be worse. She sat up and grimaced at the tangle of clothes on the floor. "I have to go home."

He kissed her at the base of her spine. "You could spend the night."

"*No!*"

They both were surprised at how vehemently she'd said it.

"I'm sorry," she said, wriggling into her underwear. "I didn't mean to shout."

"Did I do something wrong?"

"No. You were wonderful. You did everything right . . . better than right. It's me."

Besides being mortally embarrassed, she realized she was scared. She was feeling emotions she had no business feeling. She loved him. Good Lord, don't even think it, she warned herself. Don't say it out loud, don't formulate it in your mind, and wipe that expression of adulation off your face. She was within inches of her doctorate; she was maxed out on education loans, and she was starting to get tired. If she slowed down now, she'd never make it. And Steve Crow could slow her down big-time. He'd have her going around in hormone heaven, dreaming fairy tales about how poor psychologists grow up to marry handsome oil tycoons.

She dropped her shirt over her head and tugged her shorts over her hips. "I'm sorry to have to run off like this. You probably think I'm rude, but the truth is I'm a little discombobulated."

"I understand."

"Really?"

He pulled his shorts on. "No, but it seemed like the right thing to say."

She caught a look at herself in the hall mirror and groaned. "I look like hell."

"I think you look great. I think you should look like this more often. Every morning, in fact. And maybe once in a while in the afternoon."

"Every morning?"

"For the rest of your life."

"My Lord, I'd be dead in a year."

Steve smashed his hand down on the alarm clock and stared glassy-eyed at the digital numbers. Five o'clock. So this is what it felt like to wake up at five o'clock, he thought. Not something he'd want to do on a regular basis. It was still dark outside. He didn't give a fig about A.M.

and P.M.; if it was dark it was night. He'd always thought people who rose before the sun were a little loony. He rolled out of bed and staggered into the bathroom where he stared into the mirror for a while, waiting for his brain to catch up with his feet. He brushed his teeth, splashed cold water on his face, put on some jogging clothes, and tried to wake Bob.

"Get up," he said. "I have a real treat for you today. We're going jogging."

Bob opened one eye and snuggled deeper into the quilt.

Steve turned on all the lights. "Look at this fella. It's morning!" he said, giving Bob a shake.

Bob growled low in his throat and kept his eyes firmly closed.

"That's it," Steve said. "No more Mr. Nice Guy. Get your lazy butt out of this bed!"

Fifteen minutes later they were in front of Daisy's house. Steve held Bob's leash in one hand and a box of pop tarts in the other. "This is the last one," he said to Bob. "And you can consider this to be an official bribe. I expect a good performance out of you. I expect you to look like we do this all the time. We don't want Daisy to think we're a couple of slugs. Let her find that out after she marries us."

Light shone from Daisy's living room windows. The front door opened and a bar of yellow light appeared, slashing across the small front porch. Bob ripped the leash from Steve's hand and streaked across the lawn. He barreled through the door, pushed past Daisy, and bolted up the stairs. Steve ran after him.

"Sorry," he said to Daisy, "we were out jogging and he got away from me."

It took Daisy a couple of beats to figure it out. "He ran upstairs. He was going so fast I didn't even recognize him."

They both went upstairs and found Bob deep under the covers on Daisy's bed.

"Smart dog," Steve said. "Why didn't I think to do that?"

Daisy looked at the empty pop tarts box. "Breakfast?"

"Bob needs motivation in the morning."

She looked at the lump in her bed. "I'd say he's found all the motivation he needs."

Steve wrapped his arms around her. "Me, too. I'm suddenly feeling very motivated."

She knew all about his motivation. It was poking her in the stomach and she thought it must be difficult to jog with that sort of physical condition.

"How about you?" he asked, sneaking his hand under her shirt. "Are you feeling motivated?"

A thrill zinged through her at his touch. Be strong, she told herself. There were people out there, waiting for their papers. They didn't give a hoot about her need for morning motivation—they needed the funnies to start off their day. The responsibility hung heavy on her. "I'm feeling motivated to deliver my papers," she said with obvious reluctance.

He pulled her closer and kissed her just below her ear. "Bet I could change that."

Of course he could change it. All he had to

do was look at her and she felt the earth shift on its axis. "Kevin is asleep in the other room," she said, pushing him away. "And besides, I have this responsibility . . ."

Steve was beginning to hate the word "responsibility." "Okay," he said, "looks like I've lost my jogging partner, so suppose I help you with the papers?"

"That'd be terrific. If I get done in time, I might be able to squeeze in breakfast."

Big whoopee. She was going to try to squeeze in time for breakfast. Things were going to change in Daisy Adams's life, he decided. She deserved better than this. She deserved not only breakfast but a leisurely second cup of coffee in the morning. Why was she a crossing guard anyway? Where were all the mothers and fathers? They were sitting in their comfortable kitchens reading the paper Daisy had just delivered, Steve thought as he followed her downstairs.

She gave him a heavy bag filled with papers. "Since you're going to help me, we can take the car. It goes faster that way. You drive and I'll run the papers."

"No way," Steve said. "You drive and tell me where to deliver."

It took several tries before her car kicked over. She gunned the motor, the car backfired twice, and settled down to its normal death-rattle idle. She drove half a mile to a subdivision of single-family homes. There was a sprinkling of lights shining from bedroom and kitchen windows. Northern Virginia was awakening. Steve took an armload of papers and ran from house to house. After a half hour he'd worked up a sweat and was breathing heavily. "How many papers do you deliver?" he asked.

"Hundreds," she told him. "You don't want to know."

The route ended in her own subdivision of town houses. They had one paper left. It was Daisy's. Steve wasn't sure he had the strength to carry it into her house. He was in pretty good shape, but he wasn't accustomed to this sort of activity at six in the morning. At six brushing his teeth seemed strenuous.

"Yipes," Daisy said, looking at the kitchen clock. "I've got five minutes to get dressed and get over to the school."

"What about breakfast?"

"Maybe when I get back," she said, dashing up the stairs. "Help yourself to orange juice and whatever."

Steve looked in the refrigerator. There was an empty orange juice carton and an empty container of milk. There was a plastic bag containing one slice of bread, a box that used to hold English muffins, and there was an empty jelly jar. "Kevin," he said to himself.

Daisy thundered down the stairs and flew into the kitchen, strapping herself into a glow-in-the-dark orange vest. She snatched her keys off the counter and left. "See you in a little bit," she called to Steve as she whisked out the door.

He heard the car backfire and pull away,

and he concluded he was in love with a crazy person. How did all those old people stand her? He could see her rushing into a retirement home, knocking old people over like bowling pins.

He jogged home, got his car, went food shopping at a nearby convenience store, and arrived at Daisy's house just as she was getting out of her wreck.

"Now you can have breakfast?" he asked her.

"I have to take a shower and get dressed. I have to leave for the station eight-thirty at the latest."

Kevin met them in the kitchen. He took the grocery bag from Steve, looked inside, and his face lit up. "Doughnuts!"

Daisy took one upstairs with her. "I can eat one while I shower," she said.

Steve poured himself a glass of juice. "Is she always like this?" he asked Kevin.

"Pretty much. She's the family over-achiever." He finished off a doughnut and selected a second. "My dad just retired from the military. He's okay, but he's real spit-and-polish. Long on criticism, short on praise. I think Daisy kept trying to please him when she was a kid and never broke the habit. She's still trying to win the spelling bee. And she's a real sucker. If you've got a cause you go to Daisy. She never refuses anybody anything."

Steve knew differently. She'd refused to go to bed with him this morning.

Six

After work Steve stepped out of the elevator into the parking garage and took a fast survey of the crowd. Most were people en route to their cars, stopping to gawk for a moment at the police cruisers and the blonde. There didn't seem to be any unsavory characters around, except for Elsie. She had her big black purse pressed to her chest, obviously ready to pull out her gun at the least provocation.

Daisy was with two policemen. They were a study in stoic concentration in their crisp blue uniforms, perfectly creased, not yet marred by underarm sweat stains. They clearly hadn't been talking to Daisy for very long, Steve thought. She was waving her hands and rolling her eyes, her blond curls bobbing about in agitation.

He made his way over to the knot of policemen and security guards. "What's the problem?" he asked.

"You won't believe what happened!" Daisy said. "Someone's stolen my car."

"You're right. That's hard to believe," Steve said. "Why would anyone want to steal your car? You sure it didn't just roll away? Have you looked at the rest of the parking garage?"

"It's gone," she said. "It's been stolen."

"Must have been one of them mercy stealings," Elsie said. "That car was pitiful."

Daisy flapped her arms some more. "How am I ever going to manage without my car? How am I going to get to work? How am I going to go grocery shopping?"

Steve tried to look sympathetic, but he was having a hard time keeping the grin off his face. He hated that car. "I wouldn't worry about it. It only gets a couple miles to a quart of oil. I'm sure it'll turn up before long. All we have to do is listen for a traffic jam."

"I know it wasn't such a great car," Daisy said. "But it was all I had. I can't afford to buy a new one."

"I have an extra car," Steve told her. "I'll loan you mine until yours is found."

"That's very nice of you, but I couldn't possibly accept."

"Yes you can. I can't drive two cars at once. I don't even want two cars. It's only that they wouldn't take the sports car on a trade-in and I haven't had time to sell it." He turned to the policeman. "Is there anything else?"

The officer shook his head. "I have all the

information I need. If she comes to the station tomorrow, she can pick up a copy of the report for insurance purposes."

"Well, I'm going home," Elsie said, heading for her Cadillac. "I got a date tonight. I told Clarence Funk I'd go to bingo with him."

Steve took Daisy by the hand and led her to his Jeep. "We should go home, too. If the police find your car, they'll call you."

She was quiet on the ride home. She stared straight ahead, lost in thought. Every now and then her lower lip quivered ever so slightly, and she'd clamp down hard on it with her front teeth.

Steve reached over and covered her hand with his. "It's only a car," he said gently. "You'll get another one."

"It's not the car so much," she said. "It's being a victim of a crime. I've never thought about it before . . . never experienced it. It makes you feel very vulnerable."

"Maybe it was a mistake," Steve said. "You know it was a little disreputable-looking. Maybe it accidentally got towed away."

She brightened at that. "And when the garage discovers its mistake they'll bring my car back!"

He slowly drove down his street and parked in front of his house. The black car was parked in the driveway. "In the meantime, you're going to drive my car. It's worthless to me. Bob doesn't fit in it, and it takes up space in my driveway."

"Why don't you put one of your cars in your garage?"

He looked at her blank-faced for a minute while his mind raced for an answer. "The lock's broken," he finally said. "I can't get the door unlocked."

"And why are the garage-door windows painted black?"

"I don't know. I've never noticed. Weren't they always black?" He ran around the car and opened the door for her. "Anyway, it'll be easier for me with only one car." He took keys off his key ring and handed them to her. "You drive, and I'll ride along with you to pick up Bob. I left him with Kevin this morning."

She reluctantly climbed into the car and put the ignition key in. "I don't know about this," she said, peeking over the black leather steering wheel. "It feels a little racy for me." It was an understatement. It was like being in the cockpit of the Batmobile. She felt like she should be wearing a garter belt and black leather boots that came up past her knee and had high spike heels.

"It drives like any other car," Steve told her. "Just go slow at first until you get the feel of it."

She put it into reverse and peeled out of the driveway, laying an eighth of an inch of rubber on the asphalt.

Steve made a sound that went something like "Ark" when the seat belt caught, squeezing the air out of his lungs.

The car came to a standstill in the middle of

the road. Daisy licked dry lips and put her hand on the gearshift knob. She slanted a look at Steve and smiled. "I think I'm going to like this," she said, putting the car into first.

Kevin and Bob were waiting on the front steps when Daisy drove up. "We're out of food," Kevin told Daisy. "Bob ate everything."

Half an hour later Daisy and Steve wheeled several carts full of groceries out of the supermarket. When they reached the car Daisy found a pair of men's navy briefs hanging on her antenna.

She gingerly picked them off, holding them between thumb and forefinger. "I'm glad I wasn't here when he took them off," she said, dropping the briefs onto the pavement.

"It's the car," Steve said. "It draws underwear. You'll get used to it after a while."

They stored the bags away, Daisy got behind the wheel and backed over the briefs. She looked at the flattened navy material and smiled. "Roadkill," she said, driving over it one more time as she left the parking lot.

Supper consisted of canned soup and grilled cheese sandwiches—lots of them.

"The trick to making grilled cheese is tons of grease," Daisy said. "You need to fry all of the bread surfaces, and then you need this disgusting yellow cheese that has lots of salt in it. That way you can clog up your arteries and give yourself high blood pressure all at the same time."

She was frying the seventh sandwich when the phone rang. She cradled the mouthpiece on her shoulder while she flipped slices of bread. "This is *who*?" she asked. Her eyes narrowed and her lips compressed flat together. "Uh-huh," she said into the phone. "Uh-huh, uh-huh, uh-huh." Her eyes got small and glittery, and she wrinkled her nose, causing little squint lines to appear between her brows. "Now let me tell *you* something, you disgusting insect—" she shouted. She blinked at the click when the caller disconnected. "Creep! Unh," she grunted, slamming the phone back into the wall hanger.

Steve raised his eyebrows. "What was that all about?"

"Crank call," she said, turning back to the sandwiches.

"What did he say?"

She slid the grilled cheese onto Bob's dish and put a frozen apple pie into the oven. "He said the Roach didn't like smartass reporters interfering with his business, and he was going to do some unpleasant things to my anatomy. Actually, that's paraphrased. He was more specific, but it's not worth repeating."

"You need to call the police and tell them you were threatened."

"I'll do it tomorrow when I get the stolen-car report. I don't have time tonight. I have to be at a lecture at eight."

Steve pushed his plate away. "I'll go with you."

"To tell you the truth, I'd rather you stay with Kevin. I don't feel comfortable about leaving him home alone tonight."

Between a rock and a hard spot, Steve

The Editors of Loveswept Romances invite you to:

CLAIM A FREE SURPRISE GIFT...

Lift Here

...PLUS SIX FREE ROMANCES!

Detach and affix this stamp to the postage-paid reply card — and mail at once!

NO OBLIGATION TO BUY!

THE FREE GIFTS ARE YOURS TO KEEP

SEE DETAILS INSIDE →

LET YOURSELF BE LOVESWEPT BY... SIX BRAND NEW LOVESWEPT ROMANCES!

Because Loveswept romances sell themselves ...we want to send you six (Yes, six!) exciting new novels to enjoy absolutely Free! There's no obligation — they are yours to keep.

Discover how these compelling stories of contemporary romances tug at your heart strings and keep you turning the pages. Meet true-to-life characters you'll fall in love with as their romances blossom. Experience their challenges and triumphs — their laughter, tears and passion.

Let yourself be Loveswept! Join our **at-home reader service!** Each month we'll send you six new Loveswept novels **before they appear in the bookstores.** Take up to **15 days to preview** current selections **risk-free! Keep only those shipments you want.** Each book is yours for only $2.09 plus postage & handling and sales tax where applicable — **a savings of 41¢ per book** off the cover price.

NO OBLIGATION TO BUY — WITH THIS RISK-FREE OFFER!

YOU GET SIX
ROMANCES FREE...
Plus A SURPRISE GIFT!

Loveswept Romances

thought. He didn't want to leave either of them alone. "Kevin can go with us."

"A lecture?" Kevin said. "Give me a break. It'll be about old people. They're always about old people."

"I'll let you drive my car to the end of the parking lot," Steve said.

Kevin was on his feet. "A lecture wouldn't be so bad," he decided. "Maybe they'll show a cartoon."

Steve wanted to increase Daisy's protection. He wanted twenty-four-hour guard service. He'd requested it earlier from the police but they claimed they didn't have the manpower. The line of his mouth slanted down at the thought of his alternative—Elsie Hawkins. Elsie Hawkins didn't instill a lot of confidence in Steve, but Daisy wasn't willing to accept anyone else. Not only didn't he think Elsie could protect Daisy, he was terrified that she'd shoot Daisy by mistake. The only positive point was that Elsie seemed to genuinely care for Daisy. And at least Elsie was a cantankerous diversion to a would-be assailant. She was another set of eyes and ears, another person capable of making an emergency phone call. He supposed she was better than nothing at all.

"I'll be ready in a minute," Steve said. "I have to make a phone call. I'm going to see if Elsie is willing to work extra hours."

It was ten o'clock when Steve brought Daisy and Kevin home. He pulled into the lot and parked next to Elsie's Cadillac. Kevin tumbled out of the sports car and Daisy eased herself over the gearshift.

"Holy cow," Kevin said, "look at this dinosaur!" He ran his hand over the powder-blue fender. "It's not even fiberglass. It's real metal! I bet it gets two miles to a gallon. It's a wonder the parking lot isn't caving in under the strain."

Elsie had been sitting in the shadows on Daisy's front porch. She lurched to her feet and marched over to her car. "This here's a *real* car," she said. "They don't make cars like this anymore." She thumped on the fender. "This car's got substance. This car's got quality."

"Yeah, but this car's got cool," Kevin said, patting Steve's low-slung black sports car.

Elsie looked at Steve's car and worked her dentures around in her mouth a little. "It's a beauty, all right. I guess I wouldn't mind having a car like that. I'd look hot driving around town in one of them things."

"This is Elsie Hawkins," Steve said to Kevin. "She's your sister's bodyguard. She's going to be staying here until things calm down."

"Very suave," Kevin said. He looked at the Cadillac and grinned. "Are they gonna drive around in the armored car?"

"I've chased down kidnappers, dope dealers, and flashers in this baby," Elsie said. "I'll take my Caddy any day in a high-speed chase. You ever hear of Carolyn Towne? She plays the violin with that fancy orchestra in Washington. She was kidnapped by a dope dealer, and I rescued her in this here car. I wasn't even a certified guard back then." Elsie's eyes narrowed on Kevin. "I was just a mean old lady."

"You still look pretty mean," Kevin said to her, grinning.

Elsie adjusted her pocketbook on her arm. "I try to keep up appearances. I got a reputation, you know."

They went inside and Daisy showed Elsie to the guest room. Bob was asleep on the bed.

"This is Bob," Daisy explained. "He belongs to Steve."

"Do I gotta share a room with Bob?" Elsie asked. "I don't mind, so long as he don't hog my side of the bed. I'm an old lady. I need my rest."

Daisy jumped when the phone rang.

"I've got it," Steve called from the kitchen. "Let me answer."

Everyone was silent when he said hello twice. Daisy and Elsie waited at the top of the stairs.

"Nobody on the line," Steve said. "They hung up when they heard my voice."

"Don't worry," Elsie told him. "From now on I answer the phone. I'll take care of this. And I'd just like to see someone try to break into the house," she said, patting her pocketbook.

Steve walked Bob home and put him to bed. He changed into a pair of jeans and a navy shirt. He took a blanket, a pillow, a thermos of coffee, and a package of Oreos out to the Jeep. He locked his house and drove to Daisy's subdivision. As a reporter, he'd acquired a certain amount of street smarts over the years, and experience told him Daisy probably wasn't in a lot of danger. The Roach had threatened to get even, but there were lots of ways of getting even. Steve thought harassment would be high on the list. If someone were serious about hurting Daisy, they wouldn't have called to tell her about it. That was providing the guy with the spray paint and bad phone manners was a card-carrying, professional dope pusher. If the man was a druggie with a few cans missing from his case, the prognosis wasn't nearly so positive. No sense taking chances, Steve thought. Until he had a better handle on the situation, he was sticking close to Daisy. He parked across the street from Daisy's house. He rolled his window down, adjusted the pillow for comfort, and poured himself a cup of coffee.

At two-fifteen his head snapped off the back of the seat. The crack of gunshot had broken the stillness of the night. Another shot rang out and Steve was on his feet, running to Daisy's house. He pulled at the front door, but it was locked. The windows were dark. He heard shouting behind the locked door. He heard the muffled thud of feet pounding down stairs. A light blinked on in the foyer, the living room, and upstairs behind bedroom curtains. He hammered at the door. "It's Steve. Let me in."

Elsie opened the door with her gun in her hand. "What are you doing here?"

He pushed past Elsie and almost collapsed with relief when he saw Daisy. "You aren't shot?" he asked, not so subtly examining her for bullet holes.

Daisy rolled her eyes.

"Some yahoo broke into the house," Elsie said. "I got up to go to the john and thought I heard a funny noise coming from downstairs. So I got my purse and went down to investigate. Danged if I didn't catch some slimeball creeping through the kitchen. I said, 'Stop or I'll blast you from here to kingdom come.' It was real dark, and I couldn't get a good look at him, but it didn't take much sight to know he wasn't stopping."

"There isn't anyone bleeding to death on the kitchen floor, is there?" Steve asked.

"No," Elsie said. "He was moving fast once he saw me take out my gun. He was heading for the back door, and I had to aim real low so as to get him in the leg. Police get testy when you shoot a man too high in the back."

"Did you get him in the leg?"

"No. I'm not so good at legs."

Steve went into the kitchen. There was a large hole in the back door and another one in the wastebasket beside the door.

Kevin was at the kitchen table, eating a piece of leftover pie. "She's death to wastebaskets," he said. "Got it right in the kneecap."

"How'd he get in?"

Kevin pointed to the patio door in the dining room. "Carved out a chunk of glass with a glazier's knife and unlocked the door."

Steve started to dial the police. He punched in two numbers and stopped. Elsie didn't have a license for her gun. If Elsie were in trouble with the police, he wouldn't have anyone to ride with Daisy. He ran his hand through his hair and swore under his breath. "Everyone pack up. You're all coming to my house, and you're going to stay there until we find out what's going on with this guy. Take clothes for overnight. We can do a more thorough move tomorrow."

"That's fine with me," Kevin said. "I'm no hero. I'm not excited about staying here to get blown away while I sleep. I'm only fourteen. I have a long life ahead of me. I got an A in sex ed last year. It would be terrible to waste all that knowledge."

Elsie shrugged. "Don't make any difference to me. I haven't hardly unpacked yet."

Daisy leaned against the doorjamb. She'd never been so scared in her life. Her heart was still racing and her stomach was nauseous. She'd felt vulnerable and victimized when her car had been stolen, but that was nothing compared to what she was feeling now. She shivered when she thought what might have happened if it hadn't been for Elsie and her gun. She'd been lucky, she realized. She hadn't taken any of this seriously. She'd hired Elsie, not because she thought Elsie would make a good guard, but because she wanted to give a chance to the elderly. Now she didn't know what to do. A one-way ticket to Texas sounded appealing. She realized she'd been thinking along those lines a lot lately and pushed the thought aside. Running away never solved anything, she told herself. She didn't like being bullied out of her house, and she didn't like giving in to her fear. Unfortunately, she had Kevin and Elsie to consider. It would be wrong to endanger them just to satisfy her belligerent pursuit of independence.

"I suppose it would be a good idea to hide out for a while," she said to Steve. "It's nice of you to offer us the use of your house."

Daisy was sitting at the kitchen table, enjoying a second cup of coffee, when Steve ambled in. She opened her mouth to tease him about sleeping late on a glorious Saturday, but her thoughts scattered at the sight of him. His hair was silky clean, fresh from a shower. His movements were efficient but his eyes were soft and drowsy, as if the shower hadn't quite awakened the innermost recesses of his mind. He wore a gray T-shirt with the sleeves cut out and a pair of shorts that had been washed to butter-softness. She'd never been a sucker for muscle, but Steve Crow in a sleeveless shirt made her eyes glaze over. He wasn't big and full of bulges like Arnold What's-his-name; Steve was lean and hard and dangerous-looking. Her thoughts flew back to the night of the barbecue when they'd made love on his living room floor, and she remembered in breathtaking clarity just how lean and hard and dangerous he could be.

She'd spent a lot of time lying awake thinking last night and had reached the conclusion that she would be much better off if she could maintain a platonic relationship with Steve. It wasn't exactly a new concept, but it seemed to be a decision that required constant rethinking and reinforcement. Now they were alone in the kitchen and she was having a difficult time remembering why a platonic relationship had seemed so important. It would be easier if Elsie or Kevin were here, she told herself. There wouldn't be such a strong feeling of morning intimacy; there would be diversions. As it was, she found her attention focused on Steve, and she found herself trying desperately not to look like a starving woman suddenly confronted with a five-course meal.

Steve poured himself a cup of coffee, leaned against a kitchen counter, and openly studied Daisy. Her cheeks were flushed and her eyes were wide. She had that "kid in a candy shop" expression on her face again, he thought. She was looking at him like he was lunch—and he loved it. He wanted to be the bill of fare for the next fifty years. "Where did Elsie and Kevin disappear to?"

"They went back to the town house to get essentials. You know, clothes, toiletries, the kitchen sink." Her eyes narrowed a little as she looked at him. "There's something I've been wanting to ask you."

"Anything."

"What were you doing at my house at two in the morning?"

"I was worried about you, and didn't entirely trust Elsie to be able to handle a disaster. So I camped out in the Jeep."

"You were willing to sleep in your car all night just to protect me?"

"Mmmm." He sipped his coffee. "I have plans."

"Oh boy."

"Oh boy? Is that a negative reaction?"

"I don't know if I can handle any more plans right now. I'm about all planned out."

"Some of my plans don't require much planning. For instance, I plan to take you to a garden party this afternoon."

"You mean a barbecue?"

"No. This is definitely a garden party. There'll be inedible little sandwiches without crust, white wine with fruit floating in it, and tasteless cookies for dessert."

"Gee, I can hardly wait."

He took a frozen waffle from the freezer and slid it into the toaster. "You haven't even heard the best part. My aunt Zena will be there."

Daisy leaned forward in her seat. "You mean there's really an Aunt Zena?"

"You bet. Aunt Zena comes from the Crow side of the family. Her father was Crow, but her mother was Hungarian. Her third husband was elected to Congress sort of late in life. He died six months after taking office. Aunt Zena decided she liked Washington, so she stayed here. Now she's heavily into fund-raising."

"Is this party a fund-raiser?"

He took his waffle from the toaster and ate it like a cookie. "Yup. Some junior congressman from Oklahoma. I get invited to all of Aunt Zena's fund-raisers. She's decided I need to get married. Not only do I have to contribute to all of her causes, but I have to show up and run the gauntlet of eligible women she's drummed up for me." He sat across from her, slouching back in his chair with his coffee cup resting on his stomach. "This is the part where you're supposed to show some jealousy as you contemplate all those eligible women."

Daisy smiled at him. "Won't Aunt Zena be disappointed if you show up with me in tow? What about the sacrificial lambs she's recruited for this bash?"

"Hell, she'll be ecstatic. I'll tell her I'm madly in love with you, that we've already made whoopee on the floor and our bodies fit together like a dream, and that you've moved into my house. Aunt Zena will be relieved. I think she's running out of marriage applicants."

"You wouldn't dare tell her that!"

"I might."

She tipped her nose up a little. "Well, then I'm not going with you."

"Okay, then how about if we tell her we're engaged?"

"No."

"You're not very cooperative," he said. "This

is my big chance to get Aunt Zena off my back."

"You can tell her we're friends."

"Honey, I'm friends with eighty percent of all the unmarried women in Northern Virginia and the District of Columbia."

"That's a lot of women."

"I've been to a lot of fund-raisers."

"Well, it's friends or nothing."

He reached forward, took her face in his hands and kissed her. It started out as a playful type of kiss with his eyes open and smiling, but all that changed when their mouths met. His lips turned soft and coaxing and his tongue forged ahead with a mind of its own. His stomach tightened, just as it always did when he kissed her, and he felt the pressure of passion begin to thrum low in his groin. He dragged her onto the table, mindless of the coffee cups crashing to the floor, and in an instant his hands were under her shirt, kneading the soft, milky flesh of her full breasts, teasing the tips until they were man-hard.

She gasped in protest, but his mouth covered hers and objection quickly turned to obsession as desire bit into her. She knew him now—knew what he could do to her, knew what he could make her feel—and that knowledge made her wild to have more of him. She clutched at his shirt, pulling him closer, but he pushed her hands away, pushed her clothes aside and took his mouth to her, ravishing every part of her until she was writhing and moaning from the pleasure of it. She lifted up to him and shuddered, crying out in release, and at that moment he took her. He came fast and hard, trembling under the intensity of his own passion, wondering at the pinnacle if he would live through it, wondering if a man could survive loving a woman like this.

Still on the kitchen table, they slowly became aware of their surroundings. Coffee and cereal had been flung from one end of the kitchen to the other, dishes lay broken on the floor, chairs had been overturned.

There was the sound of a car pulling into the driveway, and Daisy and Steve looked into each other's eyes and saw hysteria.

"Elsie and Kevin," Daisy whispered.

They scrambled to their feet and adjusted their clothes. They both glanced furtively at the only escape route which would lead to a shower and knew they'd never make it. Elsie was already in the foyer.

"Just act like nothing happened," Steve said. "We can pull this off."

Daisy clapped a hand to her mouth to stop a hysterical giggle. He had smashed fruitloops on his knees and his shirt was torn.

Elsie stopped in her tracks at the kitchen door, and Kevin looked over her shoulder. "Whoa," he said, "who trashed the kitchen?"

"Bob," Steve told him. "Bob did it."

Seven

Steve took his eyes off the road for a moment to smile at Daisy. She was wearing a little white number that hugged her body in all the right places and still miraculously projected an image of classy respectability. The slim skirt stopped a few inches above her knee, showing off long tanned legs and dainty feet trapped in gold strappy sandals. The top of the dress was off-the-shoulder with a band of material that wrapped across her upper arms and slanted down to minimize full breasts. It was entirely devoid of ornamentation, proving the old adage that less is sometimes more. She wore dangly gold earrings and wide gold bands at each wrist. She was a knockout, and Aunt Zena would love her, Steve thought. Zena would also be suspicious and nosy as hell, but an impetuous love-at-first-sight romance would appeal to her.

They rolled through Potomac, Maryland, in the racy black car, down wide streets where high six-digit incomes and suburban sprawl had spawned the tract mansion. Steve turned into a gated driveway and followed the smooth blacktop to a monster of a house riddled with columns and porticos and upgraded window trim. It rose phoenixlike, in red brick splendor, from silver-dollar wood chips and a great expanse of manicured lawn, its nether parts obscured by professionally tended azalea, holly, and rhododendron.

"An architectural masterpiece," Steve said. "Neobeltway."

Daisy gaped at it. "I'm glad I don't have to deliver papers here."

A white-coated attendant helped her from the car and ran around to the driver's side.

"Is this Zena's house?" Daisy asked Steve.

"No. Aunt Zena has a condo in Georgetown. This little honey belongs to George and Ethel Begley. They're really very nice people. I don't know why they chose to live at Tara here."

They walked into the vaulted foyer and were greeted by Ethel. She gave Steve a cheek-kiss, rewarded Daisy with a dazzling smile, and propelled them forward into the cool interior of the house.

A sideboard held liver pâté, salmon mousse, and French bread crusts. The pâté and mousse looked fresh on their lettuce beds, and Steve took a crust and scooped up some mousse.

An older woman barreled through the

French doors leading to the patio. Her hair was black and pulled into a tight knot at the nape of her neck. She wore dark red lipstick and plum eye shadow. Her gray silk suit firmly whispered designer original. Daisy knew it was Aunt Zena from the first moment. She was a big, strong, handsome woman. Near seventy, Daisy guessed, and still going strong.

Zena hugged her nephew. "I've been waiting for you."

Steve returned the hug, then slid his arm around Daisy's shoulders. "Aunt Zena, I'd like you to meet my friend Daisy Adams."

"Daisy Adams, that name sounds so familiar. Are you a Republican?" she asked Daisy.

"No," Daisy said, "I'm a graduate student."

"Daisy Adams, Daisy Adams," Zena repeated. "Oh my Lord, you're the Dog Lady!"

A small crowd was forming behind Zena. "Is it really the Dog Lady?" someone asked. "It's the Roach killer," someone else exclaimed.

"I didn't actually kill him," Daisy murmured.

Zena clasped Daisy to her ample bosom. "This is *so* exciting. We need to make an announcement. I want everyone to know my nephew is dating the city's leading crime-stopper."

Daisy grabbed Steve by the lapel and mouthed the word "help."

"Maybe we don't want to make a public announcement just yet," Steve suggested.

A flash went off, a minicam appeared, more people pressed into the dining room. The junior senator came forward to shake Daisy's hand. "This is a real honor," he said. "This country needs more people like you—people with a commitment to ridding our streets of drug dealers."

"Thank you, but I was just driving along. . . ."

Steve muscled his way through the group, pulling Daisy after him. He didn't want Daisy to receive any more publicity. He didn't want her made into a hero. He didn't want her to become hot news. Someone was threatening her, and splashing her face across a TV screen again would only make things worse. He got her onto the patio and used his body to shield her from the people filtering out behind them. It was an effective device. This wasn't a pushy mob. These people were used to rubbing elbows with politicians and minor celebrities; they were masters at waiting for the right moment, seizing it and backing away.

Daisy didn't mind the attention from the press. She figured that was their job, just as reporting traffic was her job. For a while she was news. She didn't fully understand it, but it was okay. She knew it would fade. She held tight to Steve's hand, not because she disliked the crush of people, but because she was thrilled that he wanted to protect her. She'd never considered herself to be fragile, had never asked to be cosseted, never before wanted it. And no man had ever assumed such a macho role on her behalf. She was surprised to find herself enjoying it now.

She accepted a glass of champagne from a waitress and looked around. It was a pretty yard with lots of flowers and shrubs and delicate white wrought-iron furniture. The people were pretty too. And polite. They'd left her alone when Steve had dragged her off to the patio. "Is there anyone famous here?" she asked.

"You mean besides you?"

"I mean really famous."

He took a fast survey. "There are lots of people here who are well-known. Senators, members of Congress, business moguls, but I don't see anybody I'd classify as movie-star famous." He took a sip of her champagne. "I suppose the most newsworthy person is that little guy over there in the dark suit. The guy with the thick mustache and swarthy complexion. That's Abdul Rhaman. . . ."

"Abdul Rhaman! I saw his picture in the *Post*. He's in town negotiating a trade agreement."

Steve's smile was tight. "He's in town drumming up money to equip an army," he said quietly. "That's probably why he's at this party, and that's probably the reason for the press contingent. You don't usually find them at parties like this one."

Daisy's eyes grew wide. "I should interview him!"

"What?"

"I have the tape recorder in the car. I could get an interview from him, and we could send it over to the station."

His protective instincts were screaming to take her home and lock her in a closet, but that wasn't a viable alternative, he told himself. He looked at her face, flushed with excitement, and knew he couldn't deny her the interview. Besides, he had to admit, it was a good idea. It didn't relate to drugs or the Roach, so she wouldn't be putting herself in any deeper jeopardy. And Abdul would be cooperative. He was trying to pry money out of these people, trying to look civilized. "Okay," Steve said. "Go for it."

Daisy belted back the remainder of her champagne, gave Steve a quick kiss on the lips, and whirled off toward the house. She hadn't gotten her interview with the Roach, but she was going to get Abdul Rhaman—and she was going to do a good job. She raced through the dining room and the foyer and then stood on the front steps, shielding her eyes from the sun while she searched for Steve's car. She spotted it parked halfway down the circular drive.

A chauffeured town car drove up and double-parked directly in front of her. The driver waved the attendent away while a man got out. He smiled and nodded hello to Daisy.

She acknowledged his smile and hello with one of her own and strode off to get her recorder, thinking Washington was a friendly place and the party not nearly as bad as Steve had predicted. Minutes later she flew up the stairs with recorder in hand, mentally planning her interview. She swung through the front door, paying little attention to the people around her, trying to recall facts about Abdul that she'd read in the paper. She wanted a smooth, intelligent interview, she decided. She wasn't going to shoot for depth, and she wasn't going to try to nail old Abdul to the wall on the arms stuff. She didn't want to get in over her head the first time out. As she reached the patio, she was nervous enough for her heart to beat faster, nervous enough not to see Ethel Begley's schnauzer dart in front of her. Both the dog and Daisy let out an ear-piercing yelp on contact. Daisy lost her balance and lurched forward, arms outstretched, slamming into the back of the man who had arrived in the chauffeured town car. They went down hard in a heap on the cement patio, and in the process a gun went skidding off into the grass. Daisy saw it skim her fingertips and recoiled in horror.

Six men instantly materialized from the crowd to scoop up the gun and pin the man to the ground.

Daisy raised her head to see Steve bending over her. He had his hand on her arm. "You okay?" he asked.

"What happened?"

"My guess is you knocked the gun out of the hand of some guy who'd crashed the party to snuff out Rhaman. Rhaman's suits were all over him."

"Suits?"

"Undercover protection." He pulled Daisy to her feet, straightened her skirt, and brushed the hair out of her eyes. "You seem to have this weird propensity for running down criminals."

"It was an accident. I tripped over the dog."

"Uh-huh." He saw the cameraman swing his minicam from the gunman to Daisy. "Showtime," Steve said, taking her hand. "Pretend you're Miss America and wave good-bye."

"Good-bye." Daisy waved, smiling at the camera.

Steve put an arm around her and nudged her through the wall of curious onlookers. "We have to leave now," he said. "Miss Adams is needed elsewhere. Once a party is rendered safe it's our moral obligation to move on."

"What about the interview?" Daisy asked at the door. "I never did the interview."

Steve hustled her down the stairs and out onto the driveway, not waiting for an attendant to bring the car. "Rhaman's gone. They got him out of there before that gun hit the ground." He opened the door for her and watched her slide into the passenger seat, wondering at her priorities. Job first, personal safety second. It was consistent with the rest of her life, he decided. She'd been goal-oriented for so long she knew nothing else. He walked around to the driver's side and sat beside Daisy. "You ever have any fun?"

"Of course I have fun. I have fun all the time."

He cranked the car over and pulled out of the parking space. "Doing what?"

She thought about it for a minute. "I suppose I have fun doing little things. I like to watch the sun come up when I'm delivering papers. I like the way it colors the sky in soft dreamy pinks and grays and yellows and for a short while the world seems safe and quiet. I like the way shirts smell steamy and fresh when you iron them. I like to listen to the wind rustling through a maple tree, bending the leaves back so you can see the pale green undersides."

"What about *big* fun? You ever have any big fun?"

"You mean like a trip to Paris?"

"Yeah. Or going to the movies, or buying yourself a pair of shoes you didn't need, or taking an entire day to do nothing?"

"Last week I ate a whole bag of Oreos in one sitting."

Steve grinned. "Regular rebel, aren't you?"

"After I get my degree I'll have lots of time for fun."

"I think we should designate tomorrow as a fun day."

"I have to study."

"Wrong." He eased the car into traffic. "You can spend the rest of today studying. Tomorrow you must have fun."

She slanted a suspicious look at him. "What do I have to do to have fun?"

"It's a surprise."

"It's not something kinky, is it?"

"Not unless you want it to be."

Daisy felt embarrassment creeping through

her. "No. Anyway, I don't think I could top this morning."

He glanced over and smiled. "Don't underestimate yourself."

He was teasing her, she thought. It was a nice kind of teasing, filled with affection and intimacy. The sort of teasing people did when they were really lovers. An odd feeling ran through her stomach. It was a feeling she didn't want to identify, didn't want to dwell on. It was a sad feeling that had to do with missed opportunities and loneliness and longing. She cautioned herself not to think about it. She tried to push it from her mind, but the hollowness wouldn't leave her stomach. How could her life be so full and suddenly feel so empty, she wondered.

They parked in the driveway at Steve's house. "You really need to do something about your garage," Daisy said. "It's silly to have a garage and not be able to use it. You should call a locksmith."

"No rush," Steve told her. "The key's around here somewhere. It'll turn up."

Elsie was in the family room watching television. "You just missed it," she said to Daisy and Steve. "They broke into one of them news-talk shows to show pictures of Daisy saving the life of Abdul Something. And then they showed her with some congressman, and they ended up by saying how she was living with the heir to the Crow oil fortune."

Steve shrugged out of his suit jacket and yanked at his tie. "Didn't waste any time, did they?"

"How did they know I was living here?"

"I mentioned it to Aunt Zena," Steve said. "She must have passed the information along."

"My reputation has been besmirched," Daisy said.

He put his hand to her cheek. "That's not the part that bothers me. I don't like the media making you into a superhero at a time when some nutcase is threatening you. And even worse, I moved you here hoping he wouldn't be able to find you for a while. The evening news just told a million people where you live."

"I want to know about this oil fortune," Elsie said.

Steve opened the top button on his shirt. "As far as fortunes go, the Crow fortune isn't all that much, and my parents have always done their best to spend it."

"Good for them," Elsie said. "If I had money, I'd spend it too."

Daisy didn't think Steve was such a slouch when it came to spending money either. He bought cars and houses in less time than it took her to select a pound of ground beef for supper. She pulled the earrings from her ears. "I guess I'd better hit the books."

Elsie aimed the channel changer at the television. "Too bad you have to study. There's a show coming on now about giraffes. I've been waiting all week for this show. Someday when I get rich I'm going to Africa to see a giraffe." Her attention was caught by the sound of a car being gunned down the street. "Sounds awful close, don't it?" Elsie said. "Sounds like it's right up on the front lawn."

They were in the family room, in the back of the house, and the crash of broken glass carried to them from the front. It was immediately followed by an explosion. Everyone stood in suspended animation for a moment before reacting, waiting to see if there was another explosion.

Steve was the first to move. "Stay here," he said to Elsie and Daisy, but of course they didn't. They ran after him to the living room, stopping abruptly at the sight of fire. It raced along baseboards and swept up the front wall. It quickly gained momentum, crackling and hissing as it destroyed everything in its path. Steve pushed Elsie and Daisy back into the kitchen. "Call the fire department and get out of the house," he said, giving the phone to Daisy. He hooked his hand around a kitchen fire extinguisher and ran back to the living room.

Seconds later Daisy was beside him with an extinguisher from the family room. In minutes sirens screamed in the distance and the house shook with the rumble of fire trucks.

Elsie was standing her ground with the garden hose when Fairfax Number 4 broke into the foyer. "I think I've got it licked," she said, "but it's nice of you to come to help out anyway."

Half an hour later the house was certified safe to reenter. The fire had been pretty well confined to the living room. The front windows had been blown out by the blast and the rug and walls were charred, as were the few pieces of furniture. Gray sooty water pooled on the floor and spilled out the front door, down the steps. Elsie, Daisy, Kevin, and Steve stood on the scarred lawn and looked at the smoke-blackened exterior of the colonial.

"Firebomb," Steve said. "If we'd been in the living room, we'd be dead."

Daisy had her arm around Kevin. She was ready to pay serious attention to the threats. The phone call had been almost laughable and the intruder might have been a random burglary, but this vicious act of vengeance couldn't be denied.

There was a black and white squad car angled into the curb, behind the one remaining fire truck. A tan late-model sedan pulled in next to the squad car and two men got out. Detectives, Daisy decided, noting the street clothes on the men and the antennae on the sedan. They approached a uniformed cop and a discussion followed. Daisy caught one of the men looking over at her. His face was impassive, his mouth grim. His white shirt had lost its starch hours ago, his suit slacks had begun to bag in the seat, his brown shoes carried a film of dust. He'd had a long day, Daisy thought. Fairfax County wasn't exactly

the crime center of the universe, but she
supposed it had its share of break-ins, forger-
ies, and occasional arson. Probably it didn't
get many firebombings. Maybe the detective
in the baggy pants would be excited to get a
firebombing assigned to him. From the slump
of his shoulders Daisy guessed excitement
wasn't part of his present emotional makeup.
He flicked her another speculative look, and
she decided pain-in-the-behind was about the
way he'd sized her up. When he started across
the lawn toward her, she plastered her best
social-worker smile into place.

"Lieutenant Schmidt," he said, extending
his hand, first to Steve, then to Daisy. "I
understand you've been threatened before?"
he said to Daisy. "I'll need a detailed statement
from you."

Twenty minutes later he whistled through
his teeth and closed his notebook. "You consider going on a cruise? Maybe spending a
month in Disneyland?"

"I'm this close to my doctorate," Daisy said,
measuring the air with her thumb and forefinger. "I can't leave now. I'm in the middle of
my dissertation. And who would take over my
crossing-guard job or my job at the nursing
home? Who would do the traffic reporting?"

"Lady, you don't leave town and you're going
to be doing the traffic report from graveside."

Daisy narrowed her eyes. "I'm not going to
be intimidated by some sleaze."

Schmidt gave a long, loud sigh. "How'd I
know you were going to say that?" He looked

at Steve. "Can't you talk some sense into her?"

Steve gave Schmidt a what-are-you-from-the-moon? look.

"Yeah," Schmidt said.

Elsie stepped up to him. Her hair sprang from her scalp in tufts, flecked with foam from the extinguishers, her face was splotched with black soot, and her sneakers were soaked. "Elsie Hawkins," she said, holding out her hand. "Rough and Ready Security Guard, class of ninety-one. Don't you worry about a thing. I'm on duty here. And not only am I going to protect Daisy, but I'm going to get this guy. He's gone too far this time. I waited all week to see that show on giraffes and that son of a squirrel made me miss it. Blew up the living room during the opening credits. Some people have no consideration."

Daisy could see the incredulity register on Schmidt's face, and she watched in amusement as he lifted his eyes to Steve in silent question.

Elsie noticed his skepticism. "Listen, sonny," she said to Schmidt, "I may be old, but I'm not stupid. I know my way around the block pretty good. As long as it don't rain I'm almost as good as new."

"Rain?" he said dully, eyes slightly glazed.

"Arthritis, you ninny. Old people get arthritis when it rains. Never had it so bad before, but this dang steel hip isn't all healed over yet. . . ." She made an impatient sound and waved him away. "I got better things to do than to stand here gabbing. "I bet everything I own smells like it's been barbecued."

Steve stood in the shower and let the water beat against him. He shook his head like a dog in a rainstorm and ordered his body to wake up. Firebomb or not, this was Daisy's fun day, and he intended to be downstairs making French toast when Daisy came back from jogging. He couldn't remember if he'd washed his hair so he washed it again.

Daisy had been assigned twenty-four-hour protection. Steve thought about the cop who had accompanied Daisy on her jog. The man had been on duty all night. Steve felt a little better knowing the poor guy was undoubtedly in more agony than he was. He toweled off, dressed in khaki shorts and a black T-shirt, and padded down to the kitchen.

He had the table set and the French bread sliced when Daisy returned. She'd tied her hair back into a ponytail and her face was free of makeup, slightly flushed, glowing with health and a sheen of perspiration. Steve felt a ridiculous stab of guilt over his body's instant and soon-to-be-obvious reaction to a woman who could easily be mistaken for sixteen. The cop was just five steps behind her, breathing hard. So much for my fantasy life, Steve thought, handing Daisy a glass of orange juice.

He offered juice to the cop, but the man

waved it away. Steve saw his eyes slide to the coffee brewing on the counter. "Coffee?"

The answer was an affirmative grunt. He was wearing jeans and tennies and a T-shirt that was soaked through. He had his gun and a walkie-talkie clipped to his belt. "No one told me I was going to have to run a damn marathon at five in the morning," he managed between breaths.

Daisy sipped her orange juice. "Usually Elsie runs with me," she gleefully lied, "but I thought I'd give her the morning off since she was up so late doing laundry last night."

"The old lady?" That elicited another grunt. "You're kidding, right?"

Steve gave him the coffee and clapped a sympathetic hand on his shoulder. "The Roach trial's only a month away."

"I'll never make it."

There were light steps on the stairs and Elsie came into the kitchen. "Smelled the coffee," she said. She looked over Steve's shoulder. "French toast? Isn't that a nice treat on a Sunday morning." Her eyes fastened on the cop at the table. "What happened to him?"

"Went jogging with Daisy," Steve said.

Elsie made a derisive sound. "They don't make cops like they used to."

Steve mounded half a loaf of fried bread on a plate, poured syrup over it and gave it to Bob. He mixed up more egg while the next batch sizzled in the skillet. He was beginning to get excited about his plans for the day. When he'd proposed a fun day he hadn't really had anything specific in mind. Then the perfect day had come to him in a flash in the middle of the night. He was going to do something he'd been wanting to do for fifteen years. He was going to take everyone to an amusement park. Every summer he had the urge to go, but he'd never been able to come up with a comfortable excuse for indulging himself. Now he had a fourteen-year-old kid, an overworked woman, and Elsie. He didn't know how to categorize Elsie. Elsie was in a class all her own. He handed over a plate of French toast to Daisy and groaned when Kevin thundered down the stairs. Good thing he'd bought lots of bread.

By eight-thirty everyone was fed, showered, properly clothed in shorts and sneakers, and assembled on the front lawn.

"We'll follow in our own car," Schmidt said. "Try not to lose us."

Elsie was wearing long red shorts and a wide-brimmed white canvas hat. She opened her big black pocketbook and Daisy and Steve both jumped back a foot. "Just looking for the coupons," she said, fishing around. "I got coupons at the food store. Four dollars off admission." She found two of them and handed them over to Schmidt.

Schmidt looked uncomfortable. "Thanks."

"That's okay," Elsie told him, "but you're gonna have to do something about your gun. I'm not going on no rides with a man who's got a lump in his clothes."

Daisy swallowed back the laughter. It was

true. There was an unseemly bulge at Schmidt's waist, under his yellow jersey. If it was any lower he'd face arrest on an obscenity charge. As it was it looked like a hernia gone berserk.

Schmidt colored. "I have a jacket in the car."

"Better have a hat too," Elsie said. "After a couple hours in this sun you're gonna be able to fry eggs on that bald spot of yours."

"Ease off," he told her. "I graduated top of my class in police brutality."

"Only trying to be helpful," Elsie said.

A truck pulled into the driveway. The sign on the outside said "Dirty Dan's Housekeeping Services." Four people climbed out and started unloading equipment.

"Maybe we should stay home and supervise," Daisy said.

Steve shook his head. "No need. Dirty Dan cleans the studio, and I've used him for two years now to clean my house. Bob's locked out back so he won't be any trouble, and the windows are boarded up until the carpenter can get here tomorrow. Everything's taken care of. When we get home the house will have been aired and scrubbed."

Elsie shifted her pocketbook to her shoulder. "What do you say we haul it out of here? You don't get there early, the lines'll kill you. I got my heart set on that roller coaster where you stand up. I saw it on TV."

Eight

Daisy wasn't sure about the roller coaster. It was one of those high-tech things that curved and looped and catapulted screaming people along a gleaming rail high overhead. An amusement park had sounded like a good idea an hour ago, while they were still en route, but now that she was standing in line she wasn't sure. It had been a long time since she'd ridden a roller coaster. And she'd never ridden anything like this. She held tight to Steve's hand and gnawed at her lower lip.

"You okay?" Steve asked. "You look a little pale."

"It's just that I'm having so much fun."

"Maybe we should start off with something smaller."

Schmidt was standing behind them. His face was tanned, but under the tan he was as pale as Daisy. "Yeah, it might not be a bad idea to start off with something smaller. It isn't that I'm afraid to do this, but—" A string of cars rocketed past them. "Holy cripes," Schmidt said, "you have to be nuts to do this!"

Steve was having second thoughts too. Now he remembered why he hadn't done this for fifteen years. It was because he had no patience with waiting his turn. "It doesn't seem right that we should force Lieutenant Schmidt to do this in the line of duty," he said.

Daisy agreed. It didn't seem right. "And look how he's sweating in that jacket," she said. "We should go buy him something cool to drink. We wouldn't want Lieutenant Schmidt to get dehydrated."

"Bunch of wimps," Elsie said. "You go ahead and Kevin and me'll meet up with you later."

They got sodas and Schmidt and his partner dropped behind. "Just pretend we aren't here," Schmidt said. "And if you don't go on any more roller coasters, I'll do you a favor. I'll see what I can do about having the old lady committed. I've got friends in high places."

"She doesn't belong to us," Daisy told him. "We just hired her to be my bodyguard until the Roach is convicted."

"You mean she was telling the truth? You actually hired her?"

Steve reached for Daisy's hand. "I'm going to do my best to ignore him."

She felt her stomach roll at the contact, felt heat flood through her when he gave her hand a gentle squeeze. They were following a macadam path that was bordered by flowers and led to more rides. It was a sunny weekend and the park was crowded with kids and their parents and hordes of teenagers, but in the middle of this sea of bustling humanity they were alone, Daisy thought. People smiled but didn't stare, didn't recognize. Everyone was self-absorbed, unwavering in their pursuit of fun. That was perfect, she decided. She enjoyed the intimacy of walking hand in hand with Steve.

They had a strange relationship, she decided. Desire had come before love, although love had quickly followed. The depth of the love she wasn't able to determine. She was smart enough to know that there were lots of kinds, and falling in love was different from truly loving someone. For now she knew she'd fallen in love, and she intended to keep it at that level. In her mind it didn't seem to be such a serious emotion. It wasn't her first experience with infatuation, she told herself. She'd been enamored of other men. She supposed she'd had her heart broken a few times, but she'd never died of it. Actually, if she was to be completely honest, she couldn't really say her heart had ever been broken—cracked perhaps.

She finished her soda and munched on leftover ice. Music spilled from hidden speakers, mingling with the clatter and roar of the roller coasters. "I think I'm going on sensory overload," she said to Steve.

"Do you hate it?"

"No, I love it! I have to admit I'm not keen on roller coasters, but I love being here. I like the food and the noise and the people. And I love the colors and the speed of the rides. I want to stay late so I can see the lights go on. Can we do that?"

"We can stay here as long as you want—unless the soles start to melt on my shoes. If that happens, I might be inclined to pack it in."

Daisy lifted the hair off the back of her neck in silent agreement. The day was hot with the kind of heat only found in an amusement park. Heat that baked off the pavement and prickled on bare arms. Heat that provoked cravings for ice cream and lemonade and the cool shade of the pavilions where more elaborate food was sold. "I should have put my hair up," she said. "I'd give my kingdom for a rubber band."

"I don't think it's necessary to hock your kingdom for one," Steve said. "Twenty dollars should be more than enough." He waved a twenty in front of a group of teenage girls. "Anyone want to trade this for a rubber band?"

Three of them furiously worked at their ponytails and he took the first elastic that was placed in his hand. He turned it over to Daisy. "Wouldn't want you to think the heir to the Crow oil fortune was a piker when it came to your comfort."

Daisy swept the hair back from her face and wrapped the elastic around it. "Does an oil-fortune heir spend lots of time at amusement parks?"

"Last time I went to an amusement park was when I was seventeen. I took Jessica Mae Stiller on the roller coaster, and she got so scared she wet her pants."

"How about you? Were you scared?"

"Yeah, but at that point in my life I thought being scared was cool . . . and being cool was everything. Fortunately, I had better control over body functions than Jessica Mae."

Daisy wondered what other body functions Jessica Mae had trouble controlling. "So what happened to this hussy?"

"I think she changed schools, had plastic surgery, and moved out of town."

"Can't blame her," Daisy said.

He bought her a hot dog and a lemonade and they sat on a bench, watching people pour along the path in front of them. Daisy ripped off chunks of hot dog and chewed. "You think all these people know where they're going?"

"Sure, they're headed for the water rides."

"I mean in life."

Steve raised his eyebrows.

"They look like they all know, don't they? All these people look so sure of themselves."

"Is this leading somewhere?"

She looked at the napkin in her hand. "Did I eat my hot dog?"

"Uh-huh."

"Damn."

"I get the feeling there's something bothering you."

"It's my life," she said. "My life is bothering me."

"That narrows it down."

"And it's all your fault. You're a bad influence. You've got me having fun."

"Want to run that by me again?"

"I haven't the least inclination to go home and work on my thesis."

"Honey, there's nothing wrong with taking a day off once in a while. . . ."

"No. You don't understand. Not once in a while. I'm talking permanent. I'm not inclined to go work on my dissertation *ever*. I hate my dissertation. Haven't you noticed how easily I'm distracted?"

"I attributed that to my extraordinary powers of persuasion and my mind-numbing sex appeal."

"There's that too." She looked around and flapped her arms. "Maybe I'll just chuck it and get a job here. I could sell sno-cones or take tickets on the merry-go-round."

He twirled his finger around a tendril of hair that had escaped the ponytail. "The merry-go-round doesn't sound so bad, but I don't think you'd be happy retailing crushed ice all day."

"Lately I'm not at all sure what would make me happy."

"Sounds serious."

"I've always had direction to my life. I always

knew exactly what I wanted. I always had a goal."

"And now?"

She gave her head a little shake. "You ever have a thought that's so frightening you're afraid to say it out loud?" Her eyes locked with his. "I'm in the final stage of my dissertation. This time next year I'll have my doctorate . . . and I don't care anymore. I haven't really cared for months, maybe years, but I've been afraid to admit it. Somewhere along the line I lost touch with myself. I was so busy working to reach my goal that I didn't realize the goal was no longer something I truly wanted."

It was hard for him to believe she didn't want to pursue a career in geriatric counseling. Until this moment she'd seemed so dedicated, so enthusiastic about it. "Maybe you're just tired."

Daisy sighed. She couldn't deny she was tired. She went through the motions and made a lot of energetic noise, but underneath it all she was weary. It had come on her gradually and if it hadn't been for Steve Crow she might not have noticed it at all. Steve provided the contrast that made her see the picture more clearly.

She wasn't tired today. And she hadn't been tired on the kitchen table. She had enough stamina to run a twenty-eight-year-old cop into the ground. But she could barely keep her mind from wandering when she sat down to edit.

"Maybe you're right," she said, sending him

a weak smile in apology and embarrassment. "Sorry I turned weird on you, but I was sitting here watching the people go by and suddenly I was just about knocked over with a flash of insight. I suppose it had been lurking in my mind for a long time and I'd never before let down my guard enough for it to surface. It was like the lid to Pandora's box unexpectedly flying open and having the ugly truth pop out at me."

"Do you really hate your dissertation?"

"I hate working on it."

"Ah-hah."

"What ah-hah? You aren't going to tell me it's PMS, are you?"

"That would be insulting. Only women can make remarks like that."

"So what then?"

She was genuinely hurting, he realized. Under all the assertive confidence was a scrap of self-doubt. And she was obviously horrified that she'd blurted out her discovery to him. He suspected she needed time to get used to the idea herself before she could comfortably discuss it with someone else. He wanted to give her that time. He wanted to make her smile and push her responsibilities aside for a day. "It's very simple," he said. "It's all stress-related. You just need to relax." His eyes grew lazy. His mouth quirked into a teasing smile. "You need to spend more time on the kitchen table."

Daisy gratefully followed his lead back to playful flirting and tried to look thoughtful.

"You could be right. I've been sexually deprived for most of my adult life. It could be catching up to me."

"Exactly. If we concentrated very hard on this problem, we could have it solved in no time."

"It's worth a try," Daisy said. "How long do you think it will take?"

"Depends how hard we concentrate."

"I wouldn't want to injure you."

"I'm insured."

"Lloyds of London?"

"Blue Cross of Virginia."

At five-thirty they met Kevin and Elsie. Elsie's red Converse high-top All Stars were soaked, her hat was off, and her hair looked like it had been styled and spray-starched by Don King.

"Water rides," Elsie said. "They were a blast." She shifted her eyes to Schmidt and his partner. They were standing at a distance, watching from the shade of a Belgian waffle stand. "I feel kind of guilty having all this fun when I'm supposed to be protecting you. Of course, I suppose we have to have someone watching out for Kevin too. We wouldn't want him kidnapped or nothing."

"Man, this is the best day of my life," Kevin said. "We got the front seat on the Rebel Yell. Then Elsie showed me how to make the old-time cars stall so that we held up the whole ride and the attendant had to come give us a push. You should have been there, Daisy. Some big guy with a beer can tatooed on his forehead tried to muscle in ahead of us on the bumper cars and Elsie told him if he didn't watch his manners she was gonna hurt him real bad!"

"I don't put up with bad manners," Elsie said.

Daisy and Steve nervously glanced at the pocketbook hanging on Elsie's arm.

"You didn't have to use your pocketbook, did you?" Daisy asked.

"Nope. Haven't used my pocketbook all day. Too bad too. I'm feeling in top form, but the opportunity hasn't presented itself yet."

"Well, the day isn't over," Steve said.

Daisy elbowed him hard in the ribs. "I think it's best if you avoid using your pocketbook," she said to Elsie. "Too many kids running around."

"You're probably right. We're having a good time anyway, aren't we, Kevin?"

"Yeah," Kevin said. "The best part was when Elsie lost her false teeth."

"Opened my mouth to yell on the Beeserker and they fell right out," Elsie said. "Was the darnedest thing. Lucky the lady in front of me caught them."

"She didn't catch them," Kevin said. "They snagged onto her hair."

"It's true," Elsie agreed. "I've never seen anything like it. She had hair out to here. Don't know how she ever got it that way. And the teeth just kind of caught hold in all that frizz."

They left the park at nine-thirty. Kevin and Elsie instantly fell asleep in the backseat, and Daisy sat in the front with her hands locked in her lap, trying to maintain some control over herself. She wasn't sure what the hands would do if left to their own devices. She was afraid they'd do something silly and corny, like reach for a star. And she knew for certain that they'd eventually gravitate to something a lot closer and much more substantial.

"I'm glad we went on that roller coaster just before leaving," she said. "It was great."

"You're made of sterner stuff than Jessica Mae Stiller."

"Don't ever forget it."

He looked in the rearview mirror to make sure Schmidt's headlights were still steady behind him. "You're also made of sterner stuff than Lieutenant Schmidt."

"I really felt sorry for him when he got sick on his shoe. Do you think he gets a bonus for that sort of thing? You know, hazardous duty?"

"It was his own fault. He ate nine hot dogs today."

"It's hard to believe we're going back to a house that's been firebombed. It seems like it happened years ago."

Steve reached over for her hand. "You have to be careful for a while."

Good advice, she decided. She had to be careful about lots of things. Steve Crow was at the head of the list. He was a hard man to resist, especially when she didn't want to resist in the first place. The truth is, she'd like nothing better than to go home and crawl into his bed for the night. Unfortunately her little brother was underfoot. He was at an impressionable age and she had no intention of setting a bad example for him. Her parents were due home at the end of the week, and she was almost done with her thesis. If she could just hang on a little bit longer. . . .

If she hadn't been so lost in thought, she might have seen the car pull alongside. As it was, the first collision came as a shock. She felt herself jerked against the seat belt, heard the impact against the passenger side door. Her hands reached out to the dash. Her mouth opened to scream. Beside her Steve swore and fought to keep the car from veering into the median guardrail. They were on route 95, outside of Woodbridge, and traffic was moderate—enough cars that a driver had to be aware, not so many cars that it was impossible to get run off the road. The car came at them again, and Daisy could hear the throaty roar of the V-8 as it pulled alongside. It was an old Cadillac, bigger and heavier than the Jeep, and she realized the driver was jockeying for another hit. Daisy instinctively moved left to be away from the door, her heart beating a painful staccato in her chest, her lungs burning with each breath. She turned to see if

Schmidt was still behind them but panic blurred her vision.

"What the devil's going on?" Elsie said, coming awake.

The car rammed them again, this time forcing them into the cement abutment that divided the highway, and there was the sickening sound of metal being ripped away before Steve was able to regain control.

"You son of a dog!" Elsie shouted at the Cadillac. "You got a lot of nerve waking me up." The Jeep reverberated with a blast from Elsie's forty-five. The side window shattered and Elsie knocked the rest of the glass out with the barrel of the gun. "Don't lose him," she said to Steve. "I might not have got him good enough with that one. I don't usually aim for cars." She leaned out the window and blasted away.

The Cadillac took off, weaving across a lane of traffic. Schmidt was close behind with a portable flasher clipped to his roof.

"He'll never catch him," Elsie said, settling back in her seat. "That guy's got a Caddie, just like mine. You can't beat them Cadillacs."

Schmidt's replacement was waiting for them when they pulled into Steve's driveway. "Looks like you've been in the demolition derby," he said to Steve.

"Had a little problem on the way home."

The man nodded. "I just spoke to Schmidt. They lost the guy at the Route 1 turnoff."

"I'm not surprised," Elsie said. "He was driving a Cadillac."

"It was probably stolen," the detective said. "We got a make on it. Belongs to someone named Elsie Hawkins."

There was dead silence while everyone turned to look at the curb where Elsie's Cadillac had been parked.

"If that don't beat all," Elsie said. "I've been shooting at my own car. I thought it looked familiar."

Steve thought stealing Elsie's car to run Daisy off the road showed a certain amount of creativity and a definite flare for the dramatic. It was almost as if this guy wanted publicity.

"What a day," Elsie said. "I'm gonna make myself a cup of tea and go to bed. I'm bushed."

Kevin followed her into the house. "I'm going to call Noogie Macon and Billy Searles. They're not going to believe this. This has been so awesome. They thought it was something when the house got bombed . . . wait'll I tell them I've been in a shoot-out. They're gonna be so-o-o-o impressed."

Steve and Daisy exchanged glances. "I need a drink," Steve said. "Not tea."

He went to the sideboard in the dining room and poured brandy into two crystal goblets. He handed one to Daisy and hooked an arm around her shoulders. "I'm going to invite you into my room for an hour of television and conversation. We'll leave the door open so no one under the age of fifteen gets the wrong idea, and we'll get quietly snookered."

Bob followed them up the stairs and the three of them climbed onto Steve's bed. Steve zapped the television on with the remote and lifted his glass. "We need a toast. To a day well done."

"To fun."

"To soft ice cream."

"To roller coasters in the dark."

He patted Bob on the head. "To man's best friend."

"To toasters, flush toilets, adhesive tape, and the electric light."

They clinked glasses and sipped their brandy.

"I'm not much of a drinker," Daisy said. "This stuff is scalding my stomach and making me feel very friendly."

"It's supposed to relax you."

"It's making the backs of my knees sweat."

His eyes moved to the open door. He could have it closed and locked and be back on the bed in less than five seconds. If he ran downstairs to get more brandy, he could be back on the bed in fifteen seconds, twenty tops. He wondered if her knees would cool off in twenty seconds. Probably not. He watched her take another sip and knew he was going to leave the door open. The first time they'd made love it was a groping match on the family room floor, the second time he'd hauled her onto the kitchen table. He wanted to do better for her. He wanted soft lights, lots of time, and he wanted to wake up next to her in the morning. She moved closer, snuggling into the circle of his arms, and his heart ached with longing, not just to make love to her, but to care for her, share with her, to permanently link his life with hers. He closed his eyes and buried his face in her hair, thinking that being in love was downright painful. And to make matters worse, someone was trying to kill Daisy. Actually, he still wasn't completely convinced the man was trying to kill her. It seemed to Steve that the guy was trying to scare her and didn't mind hurting her, or anyone else, in the process. In his own mind he'd ruled out the Roach. The Roach was a businessman. He wasn't crazy, and he had nothing to gain by terrorizing Daisy. In fact, he had a lot to lose. His trial was coming up. The kind of press he was getting wasn't going to help his cause. He'd threatened Daisy in a moment of anger, but there was no good reason to carry out that threat.

Daisy tipped her nose in Steve's direction and eyed him critically. He'd wandered off on her. He was holding her snug against himself, but he was lost in thought. "You want to share those thoughts?"

"I was thinking about the guy who's harassing you. Everyone automatically assumed it was the Roach or someone acting on his behalf, but I'm not so sure anymore."

Daisy murmured agreement. "It would only compound his problems."

"This seems like a dumb question, but do you have any enemies? Can you think of anyone who'd use this as an excuse to victimize you?"

She shook her head. "I've been down this

road too. I have to admit I can be pretty aggressive when I want something, but I don't think I've ever stepped on anyone's toes hard enough to provoke mayhem."

"How about your fan mail? You get hate letters from cat lovers? You get indecent proposals from weirdos?"

"Nothing that stands out in my mind. I keep all the letters on file. Maybe it would be worthwhile to go over them."

"Anything like this ever happen to you before? Obscene phone calls?"

"Nope."

They lapsed into silence.

"I had some other thoughts too," Steve finally said. "I was thinking about locking the door and having my way with you."

"What stopped you?"

"Kevin, Elsie, the kitchen table."

"The kitchen table?"

He grinned. "It gets complicated."

"I know all about complicated. The harder I try to get my life in order, the more jumbled it becomes."

He traced a line along her lower lip with his fingertip. "I know a way to simplify things. I know how to take care of Kevin, Elsie, the kitchen table, and Aunt Zena. I can solve all of your financial problems and guarantee you a dramatic increase in fun time. And as a special bonus I'll even throw in a dog."

She hoped he was talking about a raise, but panic in the pit of her stomach told her otherwise. He was going to say the L word . . . maybe even the M word. She still wasn't ready for that part of the alphabet. She didn't even want to contemplate it. Being in love was one thing . . . being loved was another. "I don't think I'm ready for a dog."

"Are you kidding? Dogs are terrific. You can count on a dog."

"Yes, but I don't want to count on a dog, because if you count on a dog then that dog counts on you, and I'm looking forward to a time when nothing counts on me. I need to think. I need to decide what I want to do with my life."

"I can give you time," Steve said. "I can give you security, comfort, companionship, great sex, walk-in closets, roll-over checking. . . ."

"I don't need walk-in closets. I don't have many clothes."

He ran his hand through his hair. This wasn't going well. "I can give you clothes, dammit. All the clothes you want."

"I don't want clothes. I want—" She didn't know exactly what she wanted, she realized. She wanted everything. She wanted Steve and all of the things he'd offered her. And she wanted nothing. She wanted her life to be a big, blank, glorious void. She wanted to sleep, and stare off into space for hours at a time, without a thought in her head. "I'm not sure what I want," she told him.

He let her long, silky hair sift through his fingers. "I know what I want. I want you." He tipped her head up, compelling her to look at him. "I love you, Daisy. I want to marry you."

She thought back to the lighthearted proposal he'd made after they'd made love on the family room floor. She'd been able to pass that one off with a giggle. This proposal would require a serious answer, and the terrible truth was that she didn't want to get married. Marriage was commitment and responsibility. It was an investment of time and emotion. Marriage was planning what to have for supper 365 days a year. If she was married for forty years, that would be fourteen thousand and six hundred meals. She almost lost consciousness at the thought of it.

"*No!*" she said, jumping off the bed. "I don't want to get married. I'm too young. I'm too confused. I've just devoted five years of my life to something that depresses me. It's because I was in a formative stage when I decided to go to graduate school. And probably I'm still formative. At least a doctorate program is only five years . . . marriage is for a lifetime. It's irrevocable. It's like getting your ears pierced."

Elsie appeared in the open door. She had her bathrobe on and a toothbrush in her hand. "What's all the shouting about in here? I was in the bathroom and I heard someone yelling. You don't need me to go get my pocketbook, do you?"

"No," Steve said. "I asked Daisy to marry me and she got a little overwhelmed."

"I'd get overwhelmed too," Elsie said. "You're a real catch."

"Thanks," Steve said. "Have you ever been married, Elsie?"

"Sure. I've been married lots of times. I was married to my first husband for thirty-seven years. He passed away and then I married Myron Fogel. He was a handsome devil but he made noise at the breakfast table so I divorced him. I know it was picky of me, but I couldn't take another minute of him slurping his cereal milk. After that there was Gus. He had a heart attack. It was Gus who left me the Caddie. I was engaged to a real live one in Vermont when I broke my hip. I came down here to be near my sister while I was in rehab, and Wilma Nelson wrote and told me that the old coot I was engaged to had been taking other women to the bingo game in Mt. Pleasant. I guess I know what that means so I sent him his ring back. It never fit right anyway."

"I'm sorry," Daisy said.

"You don't have to be sorry," Elsie told her. "At my age you never expect to keep a man for long anyway. Men my age are dropping dead like flies."

Daisy finished the last of her brandy and set the glass on the television. "I have to go," she said. "I have to get up early tomorrow. I don't have the paper route anymore, but I still have to cross the children."

Nine

Steve had coffee made and bacon frying when Daisy and Elsie came back from crossing the high school kids.

"I could eat a horse," Elsie said. "That bacon smells great."

Daisy poured herself a cup of coffee and poked at the bacon while Steve cracked eggs into a second fry pan.

"I'm moving back to my town house," Daisy said. "This house isn't any safer than my own now that everyone thinks I'm your live-in girlfriend." She felt her voice waver when he glanced over at her. "It was very nice of you to let us stay here for a while."

"It wasn't nice at all," Steve said. "It was self-serving. I was ecstatic when that goon broke your door and forced you to find another place to stay. I was completely besotted.

I'd resorted to sleeping out in your parking lot, for crying out loud."

"I don't get it," Elsie said. "I thought you two were getting married."

Steve dumped the scrambled eggs onto a plate. "Daisy wasn't enamored with the idea."

Elsie shook her head and grunted. "What a ninny."

"I have good reasons not to want to get married right now," Daisy said.

"Like what?" Elsie asked her. "Don't you love him?"

Daisy sucked in a quick breath. She shot a look at Steve and found him smiling. He raised his eyebrows at her, and she uttered an oath under her breath. Damn him, she thought, if he'd looked at her like that two weeks ago, she'd have forgotten her name. As it was, she was only temporarily sexually excited. She pressed her lips together and concentrated on the bacon, placing it piece by piece onto paper towels. "There are lots of kinds of love," she said. "Some love you can ignore better than other kinds of love."

Elsie squinted at her. "What the devil's that supposed to mean?" She turned to Steve. "How about you? Do you know why she doesn't want to get married?"

"Something about pierced ears, I think. It's pretty complicated."

Daisy topped off her coffee and sat at the table. "I simply said married was permanent . . . like pierced ears."

"Mabel Schnaaf had pierced ears and they

grew over. She never used to put earrings in and the ears grew back together," Elsie said, buttering a piece of toast. "Everyone told her it was gonna happen but she wouldn't listen."

Daisy helped herself to bacon and eggs. "The point is that *my* marriage is going to be permanent, and permanent is a long time, so I'm in no rush."

"I don't know," Elsie said. "You aren't getting any younger. You're starting to get little squint lines at the corners of your eyes. Once you get them squint lines everything starts going to pot."

Daisy bolted down some eggs. "I know what you're doing. You're trying to panic me into marrying him, but it won't work. I like squint lines. I think they give a person character. Besides, I'm sure Steve wouldn't want me to marry him just because I was feeling over the hill and desperate."

"Sure I would," Steve told her. "Hell, I'll take you any way I can get you. Do you remember how you landed the job at the radio station?"

"I nagged you. I was obnoxious. I wouldn't take no for an answer. I hounded you for months."

"I can make all that look like amateur hour . . . if I have to. Of course, I doubt I'll have to."

Daisy paused with her fork in midair. "Oh?"

"I have a secret weapon."

"What is it?"

He ate a piece of bacon. "If I told you, it wouldn't be a secret anymore, would it?"

"Dumb," Daisy said. "This is the dumbest conversation ever. I have to get to work." She took her empty plate to the sink and rinsed it. "Elsie, I'll be ready in five minutes."

"Okay. All I need is my pocketbook. What car are we taking?"

Daisy stopped at the kitchen door. "I forgot about the cars."

"Take the black car," Steve said. "I'm staying home for most of the day. There should be carpenters arriving any minute, I need to make arrangements to have new carpet put down, and I need to do something about getting the Jeep repaired." He kicked back from the table and stacked the plates. When Daisy came flying down the stairs he was waiting at the front door. He reached out for her as she skimmed past, spun her around and pulled her to him with enough speed to make her breath catch in her throat. The kiss was long and deep, stirring the embers of desire until he was sure they were glowing hot, ready to flame. His hands gentled when he broke from the kiss. "Be careful out there," he said. He watched her sway for a moment, her eyes unfocused, and knew he'd accomplished his goal.

Daisy turned without a word. She left the house, got into the black car beside Elsie and gripped the steering wheel, wondering how she was going to drive when her body was humming in private places and her mind was filled with erotic thoughts of Steve Crow.

"You okay?" Elsie said. "You look kinda dopey."

"I'm fine." And she definitely wasn't dopey, she thought. In fact, she was pretty smart. She'd figured out Steve's secret weapon. Now all she had to do was figure out how to survive it.

It was five-thirty when Daisy and Elsie got back to the house. The window had been replaced and the grounds repaired. Inside, two men were still laying new carpet.

"The police haven't found your car yet," Steve told Elsie. "You're going to have to go down to the station and sign some forms. Tomorrow I'll ride with Daisy and you can have the day off."

Kevin ambled in from the kitchen. "This has been an utterly cool day," he said to Daisy. "Bob and I made a cake. And then we ate it. If you're nice to me, I might give you the recipe for your next cook book."

"Maybe I'll call my next book *Bones for Bob and Kevin.* Is that the extent of the coolness or did something else awesome happen?"

"Mom called. Boy, are you in big trouble. She saw your picture on the evening news in Texas. They played the clip where they said you were the oil tycoon's live-in girlfriend."

"Great. I hope you set her straight."

"I tried, but it was tough what with all the yelling going on."

"I got a TV show I want to catch," Elsie said. "One of them cable stations is running an Errol Flynn festival."

"Is that the guy with the sword and the

cheesy mustache?" Kevin said, following Elsie into the family room.

"There isn't anything cheesy about any part of Errol Flynn," she told him. "He was what you call a swashbuckler. He could have grown any kind of mustache he wanted."

"Hope you're hungry," Steve said to Daisy. "I've been slaving over a hot stove all day making spaghetti sauce."

Daisy looked in the pot. "I'm impressed. This smells terrific."

"Of course. It's my specialty." He slid his arms around her waist and deposited a lingering kiss at the nape of her neck.

"Forget it," she said. "I know what your secret weapon is, and it's not going to work."

"That's because you haven't tasted it yet. No woman has been able to resist my secret weapon once they've sat down and feasted on it."

"Daisy's mouth dropped open. "That's . . . outrageous!"

"You're going to want to have seconds, and then thirds, and then when you wake up tomorrow you're going to have an insatiable craving to eat more for breakfast."

"What an ego!"

His voice was silky. "It's all in the spices."

"Wait a minute. What are you talking about?"

"My spaghetti sauce, of course. My secret weapon. Everyone always loves my spaghetti sauce."

"Sure. I knew that."

"What did you think we were talking about?"

Her eyes inadvertently slid below his waist.

"You thought that was my secret weapon?"

"Of course not. I knew it was the spaghetti sauce. You men are all alike. You think all it takes it a pot of hot tomatoes to turn us women into slavering idiots. I suppose you thought one look at your sauce would have me panting. Well, let me tell you something, buster, it takes more than spaghetti sauce to weaken my resolve."

"Want to know what we're having for dessert?"

"No!"

He dumped spaghetti into boiling water and took a bowl of freshly grated cheese from the refrigerator. "As long as we're on the subject, I want to clear the air a little. I don't want to push you into a marriage you don't want."

"No?"

"My intention is to hang around until you decide you're going to go nuts and start screaming and foaming at the mouth if you don't get . . . married."

"And you think your cooking is good enough to do that, huh?"

"Do you want a serious answer, or do you want to flirt some more?"

"Serious answer," she said.

"There's always been a physical attraction between us that borders on the frightening. I'd be a fool not to use it to my advantage. But I'd be an even bigger fool if I thought that was enough to sustain a marriage."

"We haven't known each other for very long."

"We haven't been best friends and lovers for very long, but we've known each other for almost a year."

It was true, Daisy thought. Knowing him wasn't the problem. Loving him wasn't the problem either. The love grew stronger every day. The problem was with timing. It was the wrong time. "I don't have the emotional strength to make a life decision right now."

"I understand that, but I'm not going to let my soulmate slip through my fingers just because I fell in love with her at the wrong time."

"So where does that leave us?" Daisy asked.

He nudged against her, his mouth caressing the rim of her ear when he spoke. "I suppose it brings us back to my secret weapon."

"Spaghetti sauce?"

"Spaghetti sauce is only the beginning." His hand snaked under her shirt as he kissed her neck and lowered his mouth to her collarbone. "Wait until you taste my brownies."

She shivered and groaned when his palm cupped the underside of her breast and his thumb teased over the tip. "Oh Lord," she whispered, "I love brownies." She felt him stir against her and hazily thought his ultimate secret weapon was in the process of losing its secret status. "We shouldn't be doing this in the kitchen," she said. "Elsie and Kevin . . ."

He sighed and pushed her to arm's length. "You're right. Besides, I think the spaghetti is done."

When the table was set, they called everyone in from the TV room. Bob was the first one to the table. He bounded in and took a seat, thumping his two front paws on either side of a place setting. His ears were perked, his eyes were bright. "Woof!" he said, smiling and panting.

Elsie took a seat across from him. "Didn't anybody ever tell him he was a dog?"

"Get down," Steve said to Bob. "Dogs don't eat at the table."

Bob didn't budge.

Steve reached out to snag Bob's collar and Bob growled low in his throat.

"Maybe he thinks eating on the floor is unsanitary," Elsie said. "I wouldn't want to eat on the floor."

Kevin pulled an extra chair up next to Bob and got himself another place setting. "I think Bob's a real cool dude. I bet he's not actually a dog at all. He was probably some yuppie out jogging and aliens got hold of him and turned him into a dog." He piled spaghetti and sauce on Bob's plate. "You want cheese?"

"Woof!"

"Kinda cute," Elsie said. "In a bizarre sort of way."

Daisy giggled. "All he needs is a tie."

That clinched it for Steve. Anything that could elicit a giggle from Daisy was okay by him. He gave Bob a piece of garlic bread and passed the bread basket to Daisy. "I got a chance to listen to a few of your traffic reports today. They sounded very professional."

She beamed at the compliment. "It's getting easier."

"Did Schmidt stick with you?"

"Like glue."

"Any more attempts on your life? Any more messages from the maniac? You accidentally thwart any crimes?"

"No," she said. "It was a perfectly boring day. Thwarting was at an all-time low."

One of the workmen laying carpet came into the dining room. "There been a death in the family?" he asked. "You expecting a visit from the President?"

"No," Steve said. "Are you trying to tell me something?"

"There's a black limo parking in front of your house. It's about a half mile long, and I think it's being driven by Ricardo Montalban."

Steve grinned. "It's only a wild guess, but I'd say my mother's been talking to Aunt Zena."

Before Steve had a chance to leave the table Schmidt appeared in the doorway. "Sorry to interrupt your meal, but I need to clear some visitors. They say they're your parents?"

"Is the man tall and inscrutable? Did he try to bribe you?" Steve asked.

"He's tall and inscrutable," Schmidt said. "He hasn't tried to bribe me yet."

"Well, if he does, take the money. He's my father."

There was a short commotion in the hall, and Daisy felt a flutter of nerves when Steve rose to greet his parents. The woman was slim and elegant, from the tips of her freshly man-icured nails to the shining mane of thick, black hair. She was small-boned with a clas-

sically beautiful face. Her eyes were large and
dark, and it was easy to imagine them smol-
dering with passion. Steve had his mother's
eyes, Daisy thought. The rest of him was
Crow. With the exception of the deep lines
etched into his father's face and a few extra
pounds, they were almost mirror images.

"There's a dog sitting at your table," Steve's
mother said. "And he's eating spaghetti."

"That's Bob," Steve told her. "And this is
Kevin Adams, Daisy Adams, and Elsie Hawkins. Can you stay for supper? I have plenty of
spaghetti."

"Of course I'll stay for supper," his mother
said. "It isn't every day I get to eat with a dog."
She pulled a chair up next to Elsie. "Maria
Crow," she said, extending her hand. "Are you
related to Daisy?"

"Nope. I work for the radio station. I'm her
bodyguard."

"And what about the two policemen sitting
in that drab little car outside?"

"They're guarding her body too," Elsie said.
"They were assigned after the firebombing."

"Firebombing?" Maria Crow arched her delicate black eyebrows.

Steve and Daisy were scrambling to add
place settings and get Steve's father seated.
They paused and exchanged horrified
glances. "It was only one bomb, and it was
very small," Steve said. "Hardly worth men-
tioning." He handed his mother a glass of red
wine. "What do you think of my house?"

She sipped her wine and thoughtfully studied the room. "It's nice. Not too big, not too small. I've never been especially fond of sub-urbia and tract houses, but this house has a friendly feeling to it. It even has a dog." She looked over at Bob. He'd finished his spa-ghetti and was eating a bowl of salad. "He *is* a dog, isn't he? He's not some small person dressed up in a dog suit?"

"We were just discussing that," Steve said. "We aren't actually sure."

Maria smiled at Daisy and Elsie. "Steve always wanted a dog, but our lifestyle never lent itself to house pets. Looking at it in retrospect, I probably should have rearranged our lifestyle for a while."

"I was one of those overprivileged deprived children," Steve said to Daisy. "I was forced to spend all of my time skiing and sailing."

Maria smiled at her son. "I know you enjoyed the skiing and sailing, but I think deep down inside you would rather have had a dog."

"As you can see I'm making up for lost time. I've got Bob now."

Bob looked up when his name was men-tioned and a piece of lettuce fell out of his mouth.

"We have to work on his table manners," Steve said.

"All things considered they're not so bad," his mother said. "He's neater than your uncle Lou."

That brought a smile to Joseph Crow's lips. "I'm going to tell Lou you said that," he chided his wife.

Maria looked at her husband and laughed,

and Daisy realized that theirs was a rock-solid relationship. There was genuine affection here, Daisy decided. Uncle Lou was undoubtedly one of a myriad of family jokes and shared experiences that helped compose the strata of a long and successful marriage. By outward appearances the Crows were sleek and casually aloof, as only the super-rich could be. On closer examination there was a warm intimacy between them, a pulsing vitality, and strength—all the qualities that she found so compelling and so intimidating in Steve.

Steve smiled with his parents. Uncle Lou, being the shortest, loudest, and most flamboyant member of the Crow clan, had provided ample fodder for years' worth of jokes and table conversation. When Daisy finished her dissertation he wanted to take her west to meet the rest of his family. He wanted her to meet Lou and his grandfather Crow, his great-aunt Lucy and her twelve cats, and his cousin Danny, who was the same age as Steve but already had five kids. There were Crows spread all over the Southwest, and then there was his mother's family in Los Angeles and the San Fernando Valley. His mother's birth certificate had read Maria Louise Helena de Ortega. The wealth and prestige of the Californio had long since disappeared, but the pride and beautiful dark eyes had survived.

"So what are you folks doing here?" Elsie asked. "Do you live nearby?"

Maria shook her head. "No. We were in Monterey when Joseph's sister, Zena, called and said Steve was living with a beautiful young woman who was single-handedly ridding Washington of crime. I knew you wouldn't be living together if you didn't intend to get married soon, so we flew back to congratulate you both on your engagement. We wanted to welcome you to the family," Maria said, turning to Daisy. "We were delighted to learn Steve had finally fallen in love."

Steve sat back in his chair. He was being manipulated. His mother had flown east to size things up and see if she could push him into marriage. She wasn't usually a meddling mother, but when he hit thirty she had started making frustrated-grandmother noises.

Daisy felt the sudden flush of heat on her cheeks. Steve's parents had flown two thousand miles to meet a fraud. She and Steve weren't getting engaged, and she wasn't Wonder Woman.

Maria's eyes strayed to Daisy's ringless hand. "I see you haven't gotten a ring yet."

Steve sighed. "Mom, I hate to disappoint you, but—"

"But it was so sudden," Daisy said, interrupting. "And Steve had just bought this house and a new car, and I thought it seemed extravagant to spend money on a ring too. You know how easy it is to have cash-flow problems." Daisy's heart pounded in her chest. She couldn't believe her ears. She'd gotten herself engaged! She was totally horrified. She could almost hear Steve's eyebrows raise and was afraid to look around at him. It was the sigh, she told herself. No woman could fail to respond to a Steve Crow sigh. It happened so seldom and held such endearing vulnerability. And then there were his parents . . . they were so *nice. Daisy, Daisy, Daisy,* she chanted to herself, *you are truly screwed up.*

His mother withdrew a small velvet box from her black lizard-skin purse. "I'm so glad I brought this. I wasn't sure if it would be appreciated, but since you don't already have a ring perhaps you would consider an heirloom." She passed the box to Steve. "This belonged to your great-grandmother de Ortega. It's a very fine stone. You could have it put into a new setting."

Steve opened the box and studied the ring. "I remember seeing this in your jewelry box. I always thought it was very beautiful. When I was a kid I imagined it had once belonged to Scrooge McDuck."

"You weren't far off," his mother said, laughing. "At one time the Ortegas were outrageously wealthy."

Steve took Daisy's hand. Their eyes caught and held. His fingers were warm and firm as they wrapped around hers. His voice was soft with a hint of the devil in it as he asked, "Will you accept this ring as a symbol of our engagement?"

Daisy swallowed loud enough for it to be heard all the way to the kitchen. It was the largest diamond she'd ever seen, set into an exquisite gold filigree setting. She stared awestruck at the ring and ruefully admitted that her psych professors would have a field day interpreting her reasons for placing herself in this predicament.

Steve gave her hand a gentle squeeze and she realized everyone was waiting for her answer. She nodded her head yes because she didn't trust her voice. He slid the ring onto her finger, and her eyes misted over. It was a perfect fit. She looked up and gave Maria Crow a shaky smile. "It's lovely. Thank you."

Later when they were alone in the kitchen assembling the brownies, Steve caught Daisy's hand and studied the ring. "Ordinarily when a woman becomes engaged it's with the intention of getting married."

"Ordinarily."

"Maybe I should set the date when we go back to the table. Or better yet, maybe we should just go out and get married while my parents are in town."

Her eyes widened in alarm. "You wouldn't dare suggest such a thing. That would be so rotten!"

He took a brownie from the fancy glass dish and nibbled on it. "I'd suggest it in a heartbeat. I'm not necessarily averse to being rotten and sneaky if the cause is just."

"I'm going to keep that in mind."

He trapped her against a counter and kissed her. "Live in fear. I'm a desperate man."

"You'd better be careful. I have a bodyguard."

"You forget, I pay her salary." He lowered his mouth to hers and his thumb inched across her rib cage until it was firmly pressed into the soft flesh of her breast.

"Is this an example of your sneakiness?" she whispered against his lips.

He feigned indignant ignorance. "I don't know what you're talking about."

"You know very well. I'm talking about your thumb."

"Oh, that." The thumb lazily drew erotic circles, sweeping dangerously close to the tip of her breast. "Mmmm, I suppose my thumb is a little sneaky." He kissed her slowly and deeply while his fingers continued to massage and his thumb passed over the swollen peak again and again, teasing it into a hard little nub. He watched her eyes drop closed, felt her body go pliant in his arms. "Do you remember the kitchen table?" he asked, his words raspy against the shell of her ear.

She gave an involuntary shudder. Yes, she definitely remembered the kitchen table. She would remember it in excruciatingly delicious detail for the rest of her life.

"The kitchen table was just a warm-up. Someday when you're least expecting it I'm going to make love to you . . . on the ironing board."

Her eyes flew open.

"We'll experiment with fruit and cooking oil and household appliances . . . the electric shoe buffer, the electric toothbrush, the waffle iron."

"Oh my Lord."

"And that's only the beginning, baby. I'm going to make love to you in the broom closet. I'm going to ravage you on the washing machine. I'm going to do naughty things to you with my barbecue equipment."

They were both red-faced and convulsed with laughter when Elsie swung through the kitchen door. "What are you doing in here?" she asked. "We've been waiting forever for them brownies."

Daisy straightened and gasped for breath, trying to sober herself. "Here you go," she said, handing the plate over to Elsie. "I'm right behind you with the coffee." She grabbed the pot and shook her head at Steve. "You're a pervert, and if I catch you buying a waffle iron, I'm calling the police."

Ten

Steve watched Daisy drag her belongings down the stairs and pile them up in the foyer. "So you're still determined to move back into your town house."

"Yup."

"I was only kidding about the waffle iron."

"This has nothing to do with the waffle iron. This has to do with breathing space, making intelligent decisions, being self-reliant." Tonight's dinner was proof absolute that she had to get away from Steve. She wasn't a rational person when she was around him. She had only to look at her ring finger to be reminded of that fact. Steve's parents had left an hour ago and the ring was growing heavier and heavier. The confused joy she'd first felt was fast turning to gloomy disbelief. How could she possibly have managed to get herself engaged? She'd been so determined not to let this happen and now she was dragging a diamond the size of Mount McKinley around on her finger.

"How about breakfast?" Steve asked. "Will you be over for breakfast?"

Kevin's face brightened. "Yeah, we'll be here for breakfast."

"Breakfast would be nice," Elsie admitted. "I wouldn't mind stopping in for breakfast."

"You're being sneaky again," Daisy said to Steve.

"You ain't seen nothin' yet."

By the end of the week Daisy was forced to admit it didn't matter which house she lived in—she couldn't get away from Steve. She'd had to rely on him for transportation since the two stolen cars had never turned up. In addition, he lured her fickle brother and bodyguard to his house with food, rented movies, a new pool table, dart board, and pinball machine. There were late-night poker games, gourmet picnic lunches in the park, and midnight pizza orgies. In her weaker moments Daisy had to concede she was thoroughly enjoying herself. During more somber times she referred to her calendar and grimly added up the days when she hadn't worked on her dissertation or put in hours at the nursing home.

That's okay, she told herself. Everybody deserves a vacation once in a while, and hers was about to end. It was Friday. There hadn't been any incidents since last Sunday and the police were talking about ending her round-the-clock protection tomorrow. Tomorrow was also the day her parents were due to arrive home. By this time tomorrow night she'd be alone in her town house. Her life would be back to normal. She'd buckle down to work, complete her dissertation, and finish up her internship at the nursing home. Then what? She didn't know. She didn't want to think about it. When she tried to imagine her life beyond her thesis, her mind went blank. She imagined thirty years of counseling the elderly on problems that were largely unsolvable. In the past two months three patients she'd come to love had died. There would be more in the future. Lots more. She pressed the heels of her hands against her eyes and bowed her head.

Steve came to her side. "Something wrong?"

"Smog," she said, blinking to clear eyes that were smarting with tears.

He didn't believe her, but he let it go. He'd learned he couldn't force her to discuss her problems. After the amusement-park confession she'd closed up tight, keeping all her hurt and confusion locked away inside. Head-in-the-sand syndrome, he thought. Besides, it could very well be smog. The air quality wasn't all that great. Washington emptied out early on Fridays in the summer. By six o'clock the acrid yellow smog caused by traffic settled in the humid air and was replaced by a more savory cloud rising from hundreds of thousands of suburban barbecues. The mesquite haze hanging over Northern Virginia backyards smelled better, but it caught you in the back of the throat all the same.

Steve stood at his grill, ready to make his Friday-night contribution to air pollution. He struck a match and adjusted the gas jets. He watched the lava rocks heat. At the appropriate moment he deposited his hamburger patties on the grill and stepped back. There was a giant whoosh of flame, the hamburger patties were instantly incinerated into ash, and the fire returned to normal intensity.

Kevin made a disgusted noise, Daisy shook her head in disbelief, and Elsie stepped forward to get a closer look at the hamburger cinders.

"I haven't never seen you cook an edible hamburger yet on this thing," Elsie said to Steve. "If it was me I would've given up long ago."

Steve took the spatula with the extra-long redwood handle, the spatula he'd bought especially for his barbecue, and threw it into his neighbor's yard.

"Feel better?" Daisy asked.

He gave her a sheepish grin. "Yup. What do you say we all pile in the car and go buy some burgers?"

"Good thing the Jeep's fixed," Elsie said when they got to the driveway. "We'd never all fit in that racy black thing."

Steve ran his hand over the front fender and walked around to the passenger side to look over repairs. The body shop had done a good job. The Jeep looked like new. "We're going for burgers," he called to the two cops sitting in their car across the street.

Five minutes later they were all in line at McDonald's, except Bob. Bob sat perched on the backseat of the Jeep, eyes and ears alert, watching his family through the large plate-glass windows.

The two cops had ordered first. They stood at the door in obvious boredom, bags of food dangling from their fingertips, waiting for Daisy. The younger one was small and wiry. His name was Koselle. His partner was older, paunchy but still fit. Koselle cracked the lid to his large coffee, added creamer and sipped it without tasting.

Elsie was the last to give her order. "Double cheeseburger, lots of grease, large fries, and one of them gut-bustin' vanilla milk shakes," she said to the girl behind the counter. She shouldered her pocketbook and turned to Daisy. "I don't know why I keep getting them milk shakes. Last time I had to suck so hard my teeth came loose."

"Maybe you should have gotten a soda."

"Well, the milk shakes taste so dang good," she said. "Besides, I like a challenge. All them yuppies are out there joining spas and working on them fancy machines to keep in shape. I just buy a couple of these milk shakes every week and try to suck them up through a straw. Keeps my stomach muscles hard as a rock." Her eyes opened wide and her mouth fell open as she stared out the big front window. "Will you look at that!" she said with a gasp of amazement. "It's my Caddy!"

Everyone turned in time to see the powder-blue rear fender disappear around the side of the building. "I'll be a son of a gun!" Elsie shouted. "What nerve!" She snatched the keys to the Jeep from Steve's back pocket and ran outside. "*Stop!*" she shouted, but the Cadillac was already turning onto Burke Center Parkway. Elsie jumped into the Jeep, cranked over the engine, and was halfway out of the parking space when Kevin, Daisy, and Steve reached the car and wrenched the doors open. Elsie paused for a second while everyone piled in, then she gunned the Jeep and took off.

Koselle was a few beats behind, steering with one hand, sticking the flasher to the roof of his car with the other. He swore at the coffee stains on his slacks and told his partner to radio in.

The older man paused with the two-way in his hand. "What'll I tell them?"

"Hell, tell them we're in pursuit of some crazy old lady who's chasing an old Cadillac."

Elsie tore down the road after her Cadillac. Kevin, Bob, and Daisy were in the backseat. Bob had his head out the window, his ears were flapping vigorously, his eyes were narrowed to slits. Steve had his seat belt pulled tight in the front seat. His hand was braced against the dash. "Slow down," he said to Elsie. "Let the police take over."

"Hah!" Elsie shouted. "Them police are a bunch of wimps. They lost these slimebags last time." She slammed the gas pedal to the floor and the Jeep jumped forward. "Get my gun out of my pocketbook. Shoot out the tires, but be careful of the bumper. I like to keep the chrome nice and shiny."

"This isn't Dodge City," Steve shouted back at her. "I can't just go around shooting out people's tires!"

"Well hell, they're *my* tires," she said. "I guess you can shoot them if I want you to."

Elsie moved up fast in the left lane and came up behind the Cadillac. There were two men in the car. The one in the passenger seat turned and leveled a gun at the Jeep.

"Holy cow!" Elsie said. She swerved right and a bullet zinged off the roof.

Two black and white cruisers raced into place behind Koselle. The Cadillac cut off into a subdivision and barreled down narrow tree-lined streets. Elsie, Koselle, and the two squad cars followed.

Elsie hunched over the wheel, her eyes fixed on the men in front of her. Her knuckles were white, her mouth pinched together. "Sure wish I was driving my Caddy," she said. "They wouldn't stand a chance if I was in my Caddy."

The Cadillac turned left and everyone realized at once that it had made a grave error. It had turned into a cul-de-sac. All the cars slammed on their brakes leaving skid marks the length of the road. The Cadillac jumped the curb and did a 180-degree turn before stopping on a patch of lawn. Elsie hit it broadside. Koselle sideswiped the front of the Cadillac and the two black-and-whites slid into the tangle of smashed cars.

There was a collective gasp when seat belts yanked tight. Bob flew off the backseat with a yelp but instantly righted himself when he discovered the bag of burgers and fries Steve had carried out with him.

"What a mess," Elsie said, sitting perfectly still, looking at the crumpled hood of the Jeep. She slowly moved her head and flexed her fingers. "I don't think I broke anything."

"That was so cool," Kevin said. "Wait'll I tell the guys. They're never gonna believe this."

Steve put his shoulder to the door and shoved it open. He gently pulled Daisy from the backseat and wrapped her in his arms.

"I was scared," Daisy said. "I was scared. Boy, was I ever scared. I was really scared."

He gave her a little shake. "You're all right now."

"Yeah, but I was scared." It was odd, she thought. She'd been frightened when her house had been broken into, and when Steve's house had been firebombed, and when the Cadillac had tried to smash them into the guardrail. She'd been rattled on those occasions, but she hadn't been terrified—not like this. When the passenger in the Cadillac had turned around and pointed a gun at her, she'd felt her heart go cold. She rested her head on Steve's shoulder and let his warmth and strength seep into her. Sometimes people needed to come close to losing something before they understood its value, Daisy thought. Her life might not be perfect right now, but the imperfections seemed much less significant. There were parts of her life that were very special; there were people in her life that were very wonderful. And there was always the opportunity to make things better. Changing direction no longer seemed so depressing.

Koselle and the uniformed officers had the

two men out of the Cadillac and on the
ground. An ambulance and more police cars
whined in the distance.

"I would've gone and helped them make the
collar," Elsie said, "but I can't move so fast
what with my steel hip."

Kevin grinned at her. "Hey, don't worry about
it. You were awesome. Man, you smashed right
into them. You really gave them a shot."

"Yeah, I guess I was pretty good," Elsie agreed.

The two men were carted off and everyone
crowded around the cars to assess the damage.
The Jeep was smashed front and rear. Doors
were buckled, steam hissed from the radiator,
and the hood looked like an accordian. Koselle's
car had caught the front of the Cadillac and the
entire right front quarter panel had been ripped
off. The two black-and-whites were totaled. Miraculously, no one had been seriously hurt. The
Cadillac didn't have a dent.

"They just don't make cars like they used
to," Elsie said.

Twenty-four hours later, Daisy, Steve, and
Bob sat on the front stoop of Daisy's town
house and watched the sun set into the trees
behind Lula Kaplan's brick duplex. The parking lot seemed oddly empty to Daisy. There
were no undercover squad cars, no policemen
on surveillance. The mystery of her harassment had been solved. Just as they'd all suspected, it hadn't been the Roach. It had been
the work of a rival drug dealer who'd hoped to

pin additional charges on the Roach and get him off the street for good. Elsie's Cadillac had finally been returned, but that, too, was missing from the lot. Elsie had gone home. She was no longer on twenty-four-hour duty. At least she would see Elsie on Monday, Daisy thought. Steve had decided that she and Elsie made a good traffic team, and had changed Elsie's job description to temporary assistant traffic reporter. The town house was silent behind her. No stereo blasting away, no television, no refrigerator door opening and closing. Her parents had come home from Texas and collected Kevin. She was alone, and her life was tidy again, she told herself. The realization provoked a flutter of excitement in her chest. Even if she never used her degree in geriatric counseling, she was determined to finish her thesis and defend it. She needed two months of hard work to get the job done, she'd decided.

Steve rested his back against a wooden tub of geraniums and looked at Daisy. "You're getting ready to kick me out of your life, aren't you?"

"I need two months to myself."

"And then?"

"I don't know." It wasn't an entirely honest answer. True, she didn't know for sure how she'd feel in two months when the burden of her doctorate degree was lifted from her shoulders, but she suspected she'd buy a can of furniture polish for his kitchen table and beg him to marry her immediately. She glanced down at the ring on her finger and when she spoke her voice was low. "I'd like to keep the ring."

A smile softened his mouth. "I suppose that's a good sign."

He stayed very still against the geraniums, but it was a relaxed, contented sort of stillness, Daisy thought. Their eyes locked and a visual caress passed between them. "I love you," she told him.

"There's all kinds of love," he teased. "Am I going to have to wait two months before I find out what kind of love we're talking about?"

"You could spend the night with me and in the morning you can draw your own conclusions."

It was much more than he'd expected, and he had no intention of wasting his opportunity. The table had been exciting, but this was what he'd really wanted. He'd wanted the chance to make love to her. He wanted soft lights, candles, lots of time, lots of privacy, and a comfortable bed where they could spend the night locked in each other's arms.

He leaned forward to kiss her, but she pulled back. "There's a catch," she said.

"I'm not surprised."

"I need time to think, and I need to get my dissertation done. I don't want to have to worry about your secret weapon. After tomorrow morning my body is off limits to all of your sneaky, subversive maneuverings."

"So this is like a last meal for a condemned man?"

"Something like that."

"I'll take it."

She didn't have candles, but the lighting in her bedroom was dim. A small table lamp with a periwinkle shade filled the room with soft light and dusky shadows. The double bed had been hers as a girl. The comforter was white and fluffy. The sheets were smooth with age, their big pink flowers faded to pale shades of rose. A small television sat on a cherrywood dresser. The only other piece of furniture was a padded rocking chair. She drew the curtains closed and felt shy as she faced him. Their previous lovemaking had been so explosive, it hadn't left time for nerves or self-conscious fumblings. There were great advantages to fast lovemaking, she suddenly realized. There were advantages to total darkness, nitrous oxide, and abstinence too. She'd had fantasies of peeling her clothes off in an erotic strip, but now that the moment was upon her she was paralyzed with stage fright. She found herself fidgeting with the hem of her T-shirt and rolled her eyes in disgust.

Steve kicked his docksiders off and slid onto the bed. He arranged the pillows behind his back, took the channel changer in his hand and turned the television on. "You look like you're thinking about jumping out the window."

"Just one of many options."

He patted the spot next to him. "I wouldn't do it if I were you. You'd land in the azalea bush. Your landlord would make you pay for a new one. Why don't you come sit here instead?"

"I'm a little nervous," she said, crawling onto the bed.

"With good reason," he told her. "Since I'm honorbound not to use my secret weapon for two months after this, I intend to empty out the arsenal tonight."

Daisy giggled. "You'll have to give me directions if you want to try anything fancy. My education is limited."

She was wearing shorts and her smooth bare leg brushed against his, causing his pulse to quicken. He wrapped her in his arms and held her close. He wasn't going to rush into things this time, he told himself, but already he could feel desire burning into him. He ran his hand the length of her rib cage, letting it rest on the curve of her hip. She tilted her face toward him and he kissed her, lightly, playfully. The kiss grew more serious, but he held back, seducing her slowly. He skimmed kisses along the side of her neck and told her he loved her. His hands were gentle as they ranged over her, heating the skin beneath her clothes. He kissed her again; deeper this time, teasing her with his tongue. The kisses were long and drugging, filled with love, promising passion still held in check. He felt her hands flatten on his chest, felt her press against him. There was a small catch in her breath when he slid his hand under her shirt and cupped her breast. Slowly, he repeated to himself, but control was slipping away as arousal surged through him. He tugged her shirt up and kissed her breasts, suckling the tip through her lacy bra while he hooked his thumbs into the elastic waistband of her shorts. He lowered the shorts slowly, inch by inch, his mouth following his hands, kissing and caressing. He heard her curse his patience, felt her fingers curl into his shirt. He was half crazy with wanting her, but he continued his languorous exploration, searching for the most sensitive places, memorizing the way she liked to be touched.

At some point clothes were discarded, and he allowed himself a torturous moment of looking at those tender places he'd made swollen and rosy with desire. His breathing was ragged as he lowered his mouth to hers for a kiss that was tinged with desperation. Then they rolled together, finally giving in to the tide of passion, letting it sweep them under until they reached a frenzy of need. He drove deep into her, crying out when the climax crashed into her and a fraction of a second later into him. Hot swells of pleasure washed over them again and again as they pulsed together in a tangle of damp sheets and overwhelming emotion.

When Daisy's breathing was almost normal she opened her eyes. Steve had shifted slightly to the side and was watching her. "I'm glad I didn't jump," she said. "Do you still love me?"

"I will love you forever and ever."

She sighed in contentment and walked her fingers across his bare flank until she found what she was looking for.

"Whoa," he said, "what are you doing?"

"You're not tired, are you?"

"I could use a few more minutes."

She looked at the watch on her wrist. "I'll give you ten, and then it's *my* turn. This next time we're going to see what kind of patience *you* have."

Daisy slowly drove the black sports car the short distance between her town house and Steve's colonial, pulled into his driveway, and parked beside his new Ford Bronco. She dragged herself from the car and walked bone-weary to the door. By the time she got there she was sick, her stomach rolling with each step she took. She hammered on the door and almost collapsed with relief when he answered with his cup of morning coffee still in his hand. Her eyes were large and teary, her blond bangs dark with perspiration. She knocked him aside with a sweep of her arm. "Get out of my way," she cried, staggering toward the powder room. "I'm going to be sick!"

He swore under his breath and ran to get a towel. He soaked it with cold water and pressed it against the back of her neck when she emerged from the bathroom. "This is the fifth day in a row we've gone through this," he said gently. "When are you going to hear about that damn dissertation?"

"Today. My adviser is supposed to call today."

"It's just a dissertation," he told her. "It's not worth getting sick over. If the committee doesn't accept it, the world will continue turning."

She collapsed onto a kitchen chair. "I want it to be over."

"You aren't the only one. I'm lonely. I'm tired of sleeping with Bob. The only time I see you is when you have to stop here on the way to work to get sick."

"The nerves get to me first thing in the morning. And then I get car sick when I first start out."

He looked at the engagement ring on her finger and wondered how much longer she'd continue to wear it. "You finished your dissertation weeks ago, but you're still avoiding me. Why?"

She slumped forward and rested her head on her arms. "Because I'm a mess. Look at me! I'm sick! I can't even handle the pressure of a doctoral dissertation. It hasn't been just five days that I've been sick. I've been sick for two weeks. I burst into tears for no reason at all. I'm always tired. I'm a psychologist. I know the signs. I'm nuts."

"Is that the clinical term? Nuts?"

"It's not funny. I thought everything would fall into place once my dissertation was done, but my life is a shambles."

"Why didn't you tell me about this?"

"Because I hate being an emotional cripple; I hate you knowing I'm an emotional cripple, and I hate the idea of starting out a marriage as a mental case. I don't know why you're even attracted to me. Ever since we've known each other I've whined about my personal problems."

"You've never whined. You might have babbled once or twice, but you've never whined."

She pushed away from the table. "I'm feeling a little better," she said. "I think I'll be okay now."

He supported her with his arm and walked her to the door. "Why don't you take the day off?"

She shook her head. "It's Friday. I'll have the weekend, and then there's only one week left until Menken returns."

"How's the new book coming along?"

"It's not coming along at all. I can't seem to find the energy to work on it. Maybe when this traffic job is done."

"And the nursing home?"

A tear slid down her cheek. "I can't bear to go to the nursing home anymore. Mrs. Nielson isn't making any progress. She's just slipping away. Mr. Bender has pneumonia."

He cuddled her tight against his chest and wished he could help her. He stroked the hair back from her face and kissed her forehead. "I can't make death and sickness go away, but I can be here at the end of the day when you need someone to talk to. It seems to me there's a lot of latitude in geriatric counseling. Maybe you need a job that deals with the problems of younger seniors . . . people like Elsie."

That brought a weak smile to her lips. "There's not another person on the face of this earth like Elsie. What's going to happen to her job when Menken returns?"

"I don't know. I haven't decided yet." He kissed her again and held her at arm's length. "Why don't you come over after work, and I'll throw some hamburgers on the old barbecue grill?"

"Last time you tried to cook hamburgers you set your chef's apron on fire."

"I think I've got the hang of it now."

She loved him more than life itself, she thought. And deep down inside she wanted to believe things would work out. The natural optimist in her wanted to think she was suffering from extended PMS, or low blood sugar, or not enough fiber—and the proper diet would fix everything. A physical reason for her nervous stomach was much more acceptable to her than admitting she was an emotional basket case. "I've made a doctor's appointment for after work today. He's going to do some blood tests. Maybe I just need vitamins."

"I'll go with you."

"No," she said dully. "I need to do this myself. I'll stop by on my way home. It should be around seven. Please don't start up the grill until I get here. I hate to think of you going up in flames and no one around to hose you down."

Steve began pacing in his living room at eight. By nine o'clock he'd called the state police and three hospitals. Daisy wasn't in her town house, she wasn't with Elsie, and she definitely wasn't with him. He sank into a club chair and absentmindedly fondled Bob's head. Daisy had been so despondent when she'd left in the morning. He should have driven her in to work and insisted on going to the doctor with her, he thought. The damn woman was too independent for her own good. She was sick, and she needed help—his help. That's what love and marriage was all about. Marriage wasn't just the good times and the sexy nights; it was making chicken soup for your wife when she had a cold, and sharing a box of Kleenex when Mrs. Nielson wasn't making any progress.

Last month Daisy was the picture of health. She was a woman in love, and she was ready to get married. Something had happened in the interim to change all that. One day she'd been laughing with him over a pizza and then the next morning she'd burst into tears when he'd told her Bob was going to have puppies. He looked down at the dog. It had never occurred to him to check the plumbing under all that shaggy fur. "I made a mess of it," he said to Bob. "Somewhere along the line we had a severe breakdown in communication. She just pulled away from me."

He heard a car door slam, and he was on his feet. He had the door open before Daisy reached the porch. "Where have you been? It's after nine. Are you okay?"

Her eyes were wide and filled with tears. "I don't have PMS or low blood sugar or irregularity."

He gripped her shoulders hard, not sure if he was supporting her or himself. "What is it?"

The tears spilled out and streaked down her face. "I'm . . . pregnant," she sobbed. "We're going to have a baby!"

He was speechless. Air refused to leave his lungs. Little black dots floated in front of his eyes. There was a loud roaring in his head.

"Baby?" he said. Then he crashed to the floor in a dead faint.

He was soaking wet when he came around. He blinked his eyes and sputtered. "I'm sorry, Mom," he said. "I promise not to swim out so far next time."

"I'm not your mom," Daisy said. "I'm Daisy."

"Oh yeah. Why am I all wet?"

"You fainted and I poured water on you. That's what they do in the movies."

"Are we really going to have a baby?"

"Yup. That's why I've been sick and tired and weepy. My hormones haven't got their act together yet."

"But you were crying over it. You were *sobbing*."

"Because I was so happy. Pregnant women cry a lot." She sat beside him and pulled a grocery sack onto her lap. "Look, I stopped at the store and got some sparkling cider so we can celebrate. And wait'll you see what else I bought!" She removed a little jar and held it in the palm of her hand. "Baby applesauce," she said, bursting into tears again. "Isn't it the cutest little jar you've ever seen?"

He pulled her onto his lap and wiped the tears away with his thumb. A baby! He'd been excited about having puppies and now he was going to have a baby too! "You're going to marry me, aren't you?" he asked.

"Of course."

"Not just because of the baby?"

"Because I love you." She opened the applesauce and tasted it on the tip of her finger. Then she fed some to Steve for practice. "And

I think I'm going to take a job at the nursing home. I might not stay there for the rest of my life, but I'm going to try it for a while. I'd lost perspective on life as part of a continuum. There's nothing wrong with aging. It's natural and inevitable . . . like the birth of a baby."

Steve popped the cork on the cider and they drank straight from the bottle. "To us," Steve said.

"To the baby."

"To family life."

"To strained peas." She reached into her purse for a tissue because she felt emotional again. "One other thing," she said. "If it's all right with you, I'd really like to get rid of the black car. I'm tired of removing men's underwear from the antenna."

Steve took a deep breath. "While we're on the subject of cars I have a confession to make. I was the one who stole your old klunker. I've been hiding it in my garage. That's why I've had to keep the garage locked and the windows blacked out. I did it because I didn't want you to get stuck on the road anymore."

"Sneaky but noble," she said. "While we're confessing, I may as well tell you Elsie and I got curious and broke into your garage one day last month while you were at work. We took the car and sold it. I needed the money to get my dissertation typed."

He stared at her in shock for thirty seconds before his mouth curved into an appreciative smile. "Daisy Adams, you're sneakier than I am!"

She grinned back at him. "Don't you ever forget it."

THE EDITOR'S CORNER

What a joy it is to see, hear, smell and touch spring once again! Like a magician, nature is pulling splendors out of an invisible hat—and making us even more aware of romance. To warm you with all the radiance and hopefulness of the season, we've gathered together a bouquet of six fabulous LOVESWEPTs.

First, from the magical pen of Mary Kay McComas, we have **KISS ME, KELLY,** LOVESWEPT #462. Kelly has a rule about dating cops—she doesn't! But Baker is a man who breaks the rules. In the instant he commands her to kiss him he seizes control of her heart—and dares her to tell him she doesn't want him as much as he wants her. But once Kelly has surrendered to the ecstasy he offers, can he betray that passion by seducing her to help him with a desperate, dirty job? A story that glows with all the excitement and uncertainties of true love.

With all things green and beautiful about to pop into view, we bring you talented Gail Douglas's **THE BEST LAID PLANS,** LOVESWEPT #463. Jennifer Allan has greenery *and* beauty on her mind as she prepares to find out exactly what Clay Parrish, an urban planner, intends to do to her picturesque hometown. Clay is a sweet-talker with an irrepressible grin, and in a single sizzling moment he breaches Jennifer's defenses. Once he begins to understand her fears, he wages a glorious campaign to win her trust. A lot of wooing . . . and a lot of magic—in a romance you can't let yourself miss.

In Texas spring comes early, and it comes on strong—and so do the hero and heroine of Jan Hudson's **BIG AND BRIGHT,** LOVESWEPT #464. Holt Berringer is one of the good guys, a long lean Texas Ranger with sin-black eyes and a big white Stetson. When the entrancing spitfire Cory Bright has a run-in with some bad guys, Holt admires her refusal to hide from threats on her life and is determined to cherish and protect her. Cory fears he will be too much like the domineering macho men she's grown to dislike, but Holt is as tender as he is tough. Once Cory proves that she can make it on her own, will she be brave enough to settle for the man she really wants? A double-barreled delight from the land of yellow roses.

Peggy Webb's **THAT JONES GIRL**, LOVESWEPT #465, is a marvelous tale about the renewal of an old love between a wild Irish rover and a beautiful singer. Brawny wanderer Mick Flannigan had been Tess Jones's first lover, best friend, and husband—until the day years before when he suddenly left her. Now destiny has thrown them together again, but Tess is still too hot for Mick to handle. She draws him like a magnet, and he yearns to recapture the past, to beg Tess's forgiveness . . . but can this passion that has never died turn into trust? For Peggy's many fans, here is a story that is as fresh, energetic, and captivating as a spring morning.

Erica Spindler's enchanting **WISHING MOON**, LOVE-SWEPT #466, features a hero who gives a first impression that belies the real man. Lance Alexander seems to be all business, whether he is hiring a fund-raiser for his favorite charity or looking for a wife. When he runs into the cocky and confident Madi Muldoon, she appears to be the last person he would choose to help in the fight to save the sea turtles—until she proves otherwise and he falls under the spell of her tawny-eyed beauty. Still Lance finds it hard to trust in any woman's love, while Madi thinks she has lost her faith in marriage. Can they both learn that wishes made on a full moon—especially wishes born of an irresistible love for each other—always come true? A story as tender and warm as spring itself.

In April the world begins to move outdoors again and it's time to have a little fun. That's what brings two lovers together in Marcia Evanick's delightful **GUARDIAN SPIRIT**, LOVESWEPT #467. As a teenager Josh Langly had been the town bad boy; now he is the local sheriff. When friends pair him with the bewitching dark-haired Laura Ann Bryant for the annual scavenger hunt, the two of them soon have more on their minds than the game.

Forced by the rules to stay side by side with Josh for a weekend, Laura is soon filled with a wanton desire for this good-guy hunk with the devilish grin. And though Josh is trying to bury his bad boy past beneath a noble facade, Laura enchants him beyond all reason and kindles an old flame. Another delectable treat from Marcia Evanick.

And (as if this weren't enough!) be sure not to miss three unforgettable novels coming your way in April from Bantam's spectacular new imprint, FANFARE, featuring the best in women's popular fiction. First, for the many fans of Deborah Smith, we have her deeply moving and truly memorable historical **BELOVED WOMAN**. This is the glorious story of a remarkable Cherokee woman, Katherine Blue Song, and an equally remarkable frontiersman Justis Gallatin. Then, making her debut with FANFARE, Jessica Bryan brings you a spellbinding historical fantasy, **ACROSS A WINE-DARK SEA**. This story has already wowed *Rendezvous* magazine, which called Jessica Bryan "a super storyteller" and raved about the book, describing it as "different, exciting, excellent . . ." The critically-acclaimed Virginia Brown takes readers back to the wildest days of the Wild West for a fabulous and heartwarming love story in **RIVER'S DREAM**.

All in all, a terrific month of reading in store for you from FANFARE and LOVESWEPT!

Sincerely,

Carolyn Nichols

Carolyn Nichols,
Publisher,
LOVESWEPT
Bantam Books
666 Fifth Avenue
New York, NY 10103

THE LATEST IN BOOKS
AND AUDIO CASSETTES

60 Minutes to a Better, More Beautiful You!

Now it's easier than ever to awaken your sensuality, stay slim forever—even make yourself irresistible. With Bantam's bestselling subliminal audio tapes, you're only 60 minutes away from a better, more beautiful you!

__ 45004-2	**Slim Forever**	$8.95
__ 45035-2	**Stop Smoking Forever**	$8.95
__ 45022-0	**Positively Change Your Life**	$8.95
__ 45041-7	**Stress Free Forever**	$8.95
__ 45106-5	**Get a Good Night's Sleep**	$7.95
__ 45094-8	**Improve Your Concentration**	$7.95
__ 45172-3	**Develop A Perfect Memory**	$8.95

Bantam Books, Dept. LT, 414 East Golf Road, Des Plaines, IL 60016

Please send me the items I have checked above. I am enclosing $_____ (please add $2.50 to cover postage and handling). Send check or money order, no cash or C.O.D.s please. (Tape offer good in USA only.)

Mr/Ms _____

Address _____

City/State _____ Zip _____

LT-2/91

Please allow four to six weeks for delivery.
Prices and availability subject to change without notice.